Nigel Pluckrose:

Please Sit Down

Benjamin Bright

PublishAmerica

Baltimore

First printing

ISBN: 1-4137-0036-5
PUBLISHED BY PUBLISHAMERICA, LLLP
www.publishamerica.com
Baltimore

Printed in the United States of America

Dedication

I would like to dedicate this book to the following;

My very first friend, Nigel Pluckrose, God Bless You.

My loving wife, Christine, whose support and encouragement has never wavered.

And to a gentleman, who had an anonymous lunch with me. A man who made me feel that I was not crazy. Whose soul touched mine and changed it forever, with a smile and a laugh, he showed me that dreams do come true.
Thank you "Tif"

Acknowledgements

I would be extremely remiss if I did not acknowledge the following people for the support that they have shown me over the years, through laughter, love and mayhem.

My Parents and Sisters

My Kids; Dallas, Chantel, Tonia, Darryl, Sam and Zach

"Gord"

Sandra (Lola) Baker

Jen Frankel

John Mercer

John Foster

Michael Huber

All my kids from 14 years of coaching soccer

Table of Contents

From Nigel Pluckrose

Hi Reader, welcome to my book.

Before we get to the stories, I would like to tell you who I was and where I lived as a young boy. But if I did, then where would the mystery be?

Maybe I could tell you about the pets that I grew up with. But then you wouldn't be able to discover their secrets, would you?

Hmm…let's see, what can I say that will help you? Hey, I know….

My name is Nigel Pluckrose and I when was between three and ten years old, I grew up in a very small village in the English countryside called Southwater. Our village was so small that they took away our train tracks because not enough people used the train.

Anyway, to find where I lived was not that hard. All you have to do is turn West at the old train-bridge and follow the narrow road out of the village. Go past the Village Common and the cricket field, keep going past the old stone church with the low stone wall and the high Belfry. Pretty soon you will come to a very steep hill, halfway down the hill there is a curve which has an even narrower lane leading from it, called Two-Mile Lane, off around another turn. Take that small lane.

Once you are around the corner, hedges close in the sides of the lane and the trees grow over the top to block out the sunlight. It's almost like going into a big tunnel. Follow the lane, which will turn to dirt soon. You will pass through two farmyards, so watch where you walk or you may get something on your shoe. After you pass through the second farmyard you will see a gate with a sign on it that reads "Carpenter's Kennels". You have reached the end of the lane and that's my house in front of you.

It's a very big house that is all on one floor, has no basement and is over one hundred years old. It is shaped like a giant "L" with green tin walls and a red tin roof. Each room has its own fireplace because the house didn't have a furnace and it has a white veranda that is eight feet wide, that runs along the entire length of the "L". My little sister, Johanna (Joey), is four now and we ride our bikes along the veranda when it rains.

My older brother, Norman, has a bedroom beside mine. He is ten and says that I bother him. Joey and I try to stay out of his way, as he is mean to us sometimes.

Mom works looking after the Kennels where we keep our sixty-five dogs, plus the border dogs that stay with us. Then she has to look after our forty-five cats. It's a lot of work for her, so we usually only see her at supper. Dad works in London. It's a long way to go, so he gets home late and on the weekends he has to help in the Kennels and takes our dogs to dog shows. When he has time he shows me how to do stuff, which usually ends up getting me in trouble. Like when he taught me to drive the car, that was not such a good idea.

Granny is my dad's mother and she looks after us almost all the time. She is from Wales and is very small and old, with her gray hair under her hair net. She always wore an apron and a smile. We had a pet graveyard under her bedroom window where she helped me bury my Hamster.

Behind our house was a large forest, over a thousand acres. That's where I went to play. Nobody else lived near the forest, except for the hermit, Loopy Lou. But he lived way over on the other side so I rarely saw him. My dad said "nothing can happen" in the forest and as long as I came home for lunch and supper, then I could play there. Also, he said that it was all right for me to go up to the farm to play with Michael if I didn't bother Mr. Day and his farmhand Chris.

Michael and I were not allowed to play together very often as we usually got into a lot of trouble. But not all of it was my fault; you see I am kind of blind in one eye and have a really short attention span, so I get bored very quickly. Mom says that I am hyperactive and need to learn to sit still. Dad says that I just have an active imagination and will grow out of it one day. My doctor says that I'm ADD and ADHD.

Me, I'm not sure. All I know is that other kids pick on me because I'm different. They always pick me last for any team and then complain that I can't do anything right. But I didn't care too much; I have the forest, the farm and my freedom.

So there you have it. That's about all I can tell you for now. The rest is for you to discover in my stories.

Remember; all the animals are real, they were my pets and I loved each of them. Also, please don't try any of the things I did as you may not be as lucky as me and you might get hurt.

Thanks. Hope you enjoy discovering my world as much as I did.

Sincerely,

Nigel Pluckrose

A Playmate Lost

"Because you are always complaining that you have no one to play with."

My mother had just finished explaining why she had invited her friend's son over to our house. No wonder I had no playmates, look where we lived. I was seven years old and not impressed with this kid.

By now we lived in an old Victorian house in the English countryside. The house was in the shape of an L and had one floor. It was surrounded by ten acres of property that was split into horse paddocks, dog and cat kennels, chicken coops and woods.

Our property was in turn closed off from the world at the rear by a thousand-acre forest that had wide paths cut through it. Closing off the front was a seven hundred-acre farm and beyond that was another three hundred-acre farm.

In order to come to our place, a mile long lane that snaked its way through the two farmyards had to be navigated.

The house had six rooms along one wing and five rooms contained in the other. Each room was twelve feet wide, sixteen feet long, had a ten-foot ceiling and a large fireplace to ward off the spring dampness. There was a window in the back wall and a door in the opposite wall that exited to a covered, eight-foot wide veranda.

Doors connected adjacent rooms. The washrooms were

little rooms at the end of each wing. We had no indoor plumbing, but we did have half a forty-five gallon drum with a toilet seat on the top in each small room. At night you knew that it was haunted, it had to be.

At this point in my life, I was not allowed to play with the kid from the farm above us. The reason given by our parents was very simple. "You kids get in too much trouble together."

This speech was given after an incident that included a hay barn, an innocent fire, an emergency exit and a pitchfork. (Don't ask.)

During this period of punishment we were encouraged to go for walks in the forest. As my father would say, "Why don't you go play in the forest?"

The forest had been discovered already and I knew all the paths, rivers, fox and badger holes that there were. I also found where the hermit lived. There was nothing new to discover and I was really quite bored.

The boy coming to play was one of those kids that others tried to avoid. He really was a pain in the butt. He knew everything and was always impeccably dressed. It wasn't that he was boring (even if he was), he was just a plain pain in the butt.

I was not looking forward to this, but I was already in enough trouble after the barn, so I conceded to my mother's wishes. But I didn't have to enjoy it and he was going to do what I wanted.

It had rained all night and I was excited about the event that I had been planning for just such a day.

When Gregory arrived, I was busy pulling the old bike

out of the pile of junk behind the barn.

He was dressed in clothes that had been pressed, had his slicked down hair combed properly, a raincoat and rubber boots. As we were being introduced he put out his hand to shake mine. In a very nice, polite voice he said, "Very nice to meet you."

My mother was watching me intently.

"And you," I answered as politely as my gritted teeth would allow.

Our mothers smiled at each other, both proud of their children's manners.

"May we go play in the forest, please?" I asked my mother. Gregory's mother got a look of apprehension.

My mother explained to her that we would be fine. "They can't get in to any trouble. They go exploring, and there are seldom people. They will be fine."

His mother tentatively consented, but added, "Be good and be careful. We have to go to Auntie's for tea later, so try not to get dirty."

I was already running at full tilt towards the old barn. "Come on!" I yelled. Gregory started walking after me.

I didn't have to turn around to receive the warning. I could feel my mother's eyes boring into the back of my head as she silently prayed to her God that everything would be all right.

It wasn't that I was a bad child. I liked the way my father put it best. "The boy has an active imagination." He always seemed to have to explain to people, after apologizing for another one of my escapades.

"Careful dear," Gregory's mother called out.

"Don't worry," I shouted back, "I'll look after him."

Somehow I knew that was what my mother was secretly afraid of.

I was uncovering the old bike from the junk pile when Gregory finally got to the barn.

"I thought we were going to explore in the forest," Gregory said.

"No," I replied, "we are allowed to play in the forest, but we need something to play with. Help me pull this bike out."

"It's broken, why do you want it?" he questioned.

"I'm going to test it," I announced. I had come up with the idea after watching one of our dogs. The dog had run down a hill on one of the forest paths. As the hill was very steep, the dog could not stop or make the turn at the bottom. It had plunged in to a river at the bottom.

I had laughed at the time, but then I had discovered the old bike. It had all made logical sense to me. I was grounded from my bike, but this was not my bike, and nobody wanted it.

He stood with his arms folded and watched as I struggled with it.

"You going to help?"

"I'm not allowed to get dirty."

He was getting on my nerves already. "Fine, but I've been waiting to do this and today is the kind of day I've been waiting for."

After another twenty minutes of struggling, I managed to free my prize. It was a grand bike, a little too big for me but it would have been great for the adult who had owned it. The green paint was rusted in some spots and scraped off in others. The tires had been taken off, but the metal rims looked fine and most of the spokes were still in place. The seat was loose, the handle was bent to the left and the chain was off.

Perfect.

Pushing the bike, I headed to the forest with Gregory following.

"Wait for me." My little sister was running to catch up. When she saw the bike she started, "I'm telling. You're not allowed to ride your bike."

"It's not mine and nobody wants it. You be quiet or you can't play with us."

"Mom said I could."

"Well, we're playing with this. You want to help?"

"Sure."

Little sisters are easy to deal with at that age.

The gate that blocked the entrance to the woods was locked. Leaning the bike against it, I climbed on top. With Johanna pushing and me pulling, we managed to get the bike balanced on the top. One last push and it crashed to the ground on the other side.

Gregory stood watching. He was not allowed to get dirty.

It was not very far to the hill. Standing at the top it looked a little steep.

It was.

The path was about sixteen feet wide. On both sides grew tall pine trees. The slope was gentle at the top, then got steeper, then, really dropped off at quite an incline.

At the base of the hill, the path made a ninety degree

turn to the right, and had steps that went down to a small bridge. A river ran across the base of the hill and the game warden had built a pole rail, out of a young tree, between the river and the path.

Standing at the top of the hill you could not see the railing or the bridge to the right.

The grass grew about three feet from the forest on either side of the path, but the center of the path was made of red clay about fifteen feet wide, that ran down the entire length.

The rain always made the clay really slick and when you walked on it, it stuck to your boots in clumps that made it hard to walk.

Turning the bike on the seat and handle bars, I started to put the chain on. Johanna went off to pick flowers nearby. Gregory stood there with his arms folded, watching.

Spinning the pedals, I was satisfied that the chain was fine. Flipping the bike over, I managed to get Gregory to at least hold it upright while I straightened the handle bar.

The front wheel held between my legs and using all my strength, I got them straight enough to ride. Still, they were pointing to the side but it would have to do.

Gregory looked at me. "Now what?"

He had no sense of adventure, this kid. "Now I ride it down the hill and over the bridge."

"That's it?" he asked.

Pushing the bike to the crest of the hill, I was ignoring him. I had been waiting for this day for a week. No snot-nosed, stuck up, know-it-all was going to ruin it. I knew that I could make that turn at the bottom. I would be famous, even if I was the only one who knew it.

Standing at the crest, I prepared for my first run at destiny.

"I'll go first," Gregory stated.

"What?"

"I'll go first, or would you rather I told your mother that you wouldn't let me play." He stood with his arms folded, waiting for my answer. I was already in enough trouble, so it was easy to agree to his terms. But, I didn't like it.

Holding the bike upright, I was giving instructions as he climbed aboard.

"Go straight down the middle, at the bottom turn right. You will have to go down about five steps, then turn left. Ride over the bridge and wait on the other side. I'll help push the bike back up."

Gregory had his instructions. Johanna wanted hers. "You stand right here and when I tell you, say 'go'."

Sitting on the bike, Gregory had to lean forward to reach the handle bar. He had his right arm straight and the left one bent in as he held the steering. However, he could not reach the pedals.

Off he got and I yanked the old seat out of its hole. He got back on. That was much better. He still had one arm bent and the other straight to accommodate the crooked steering but now he could pedal, as long as he stood up.

"Ready?" I asked. He was looking straight down the path and nodded.

"GO!" yelled Johanna, pleased with her part and jumping up and down in excitement.

We had started the bike on a grassy part of the path. As

he pumped the pedals, I ran beside him pushing to help get the speed up. Finally there was enough speed that he was pulling away from me. Over the crest of the hill he went, I stopped at the top to watch him go.

Suddenly, I was getting very angry. He had stolen my glory. All he had to do was get over the bridge and it was not worth me trying, he would be famous, not me.

He had arrived at the clay part of the hill and was starting to pick up speed. The ride was bumpier than I had thought and he yelled, in pain, as the seat post slammed into his butt.

I was amazed at how much speed he was picking up.

The clay was sticking to the rims. Lumps of red, sticky clay were flying up from the back wheel and pasting themselves to his back and head. There were also lumps coming up from the front rim. These were hitting him in the chest and face. He was still picking up speed.

He was three quarters of the way down, when he yelled something.

Without turning, I asked Johanna what he said.

"No brakes," came the monotone answer.

We could do nothing but stand and watch him go. It really was incredible that he was still on it.

Arriving at the bottom of the hill he turned the handle bar to steer around the corner.

There was another yell, this one of surprise, as the wheel rim dug sideways into the clay and catapulted Gregory in to the air. He flew over the rail and landed with a splash in the middle of the shallow river.

The back end of the bike hit the cross rail, and then the

rest of it skidded under the rail and landed beside him with another splash.

"Oh, oh." I looked down at my sister as she finished, "You are in trouble."

We both ran down the hill, on the grassy side of course. Gregory had not moved from where he had landed. He just sat there in the middle of the river, soaking wet, covered with red clay and a stunned look on his face.

"Almost," I said. It was my way of telling him what a good job he had done.

He had tears forming in his eyes as he looked at us. "I'm not allowed to get dirty."

"No problem," I reassured him.

We dragged him out of the river and pulled him back up the hill, leaving the old bike where it was, for now.

Sticking to the back of the house, we made our way to the hose without being seen. It took about a half- hour, but we got the clay hosed off him. That's when my mother arrived. Johanna beat a hasty retreat.

"What is going on?" She was getting that look in her eyes.

"Gregory, you are all wet!" She was also starting to state the obvious.

"But not dirty," I stated, smiling as innocently as possible and holding up my index finger to punctuate the point.

That night as I lay in my room, my stomach growling from lack of food and my butt hurting from the spanking, Johanna came in with some cookies she had stolen.

"Here, I hate going to bed without supper too. Gregory's mom said he can't come over to play anymore." She left and went back to her bed.

All things considered it had been a good day. What was I going to do tomorrow with nobody to play with again? Well, the bike had to be rescued.

Gypsies

It had been a grand day. There had been a morning exploring the forest and an afternoon working on the tree house. For a seven-year-old, this was a great place to live at the best of times and a jail cell any other time.

Most days I was hungry when I went to bed. Not because we lacked food but as punishment for some crime that I had committed. Usually, because I didn't know it was a punishable offence, I would end up telling on myself. But this had been a grand day.

I was laying in bed dreaming of adventures that could be accomplished the next day and my belly was so full of Granny's trifle that I could still taste it, or maybe I didn't brush my teeth.

When I woke up, I had goose bumps and a feeling that I was being watched.

Laying in the dark, I pulled the covers over my ears so that only the top of my head and eyes were visible (you never know when your ear will be yanked off or where an earwig might crawl in to).

There were shapes in the darkness that I recognized, but nothing that wasn't supposed to be there. No strange sounds like chains or thumping. No goblins, fairies or ghosts. Not even my brother Norman trying to scare me again. Nothing, just darkness and my stuff.

Still scanning the room, I scolded myself out loud. "You're being stupid, there's nothing going to get you."

I let out a slow breath as nothing jumped out to rip off my ear. Feeling rather embarrassed at my fear I settled down to sleep again.

That was when I noticed the light for the first time.

My curtains were closed, but the bright bluish white beams were poking through some of the cracks. I had no fear, because it was just light, but it wasn't supposed to be there. As I curiously wondered where it was coming from, they appeared to get fainter.

This was too much for me to take. Climbing out of bed, I made sure that I couched as I approached the window. The rays of light were almost gone as I reached up and started to part the curtains. There was enough of a gap for me to look through with one eye. Nothing, just a bluish, white light that was strangely moving away down the backside of the house.

This was something new.

This had to be investigated and I was just the man for the job. Excitedly I pulled on my old jeans and a sweater over my pajamas, then socks and my running shoes.

I ran across the room to the door and stopped. It was only a light, nothing to be afraid of, but just in case. Running back to the fireplace, I grabbed my bow and arrows.

This was the weapon I had made when playing Robin Hood and his Merry Men. It was more like Robin Hood, but I did have a very accurate weapon, as long as the arrow was straight. I hung the bow across my shoulders and chest;

the arrows were tucked into my belt.

Now I was ready.

I ran out the door and headed down the veranda to the corner were the two wings met. There was a small porch way here that led to the back garden and the animals. As I walked through the light was moving beyond the trees.

It was in the forest.

Running down the back garden path and past the dogs, cats, chickens, goat, cow, horse and greenhouses, only one dog barked. A perfect start.

Nobody knew I was gone, they were all sleeping.

When I reached the back fence, by the big, old Oak tree, the light was stopped in one place. I still could not see what it was, but I could tell in what direction it was coming from.

Now I was nervous. I had not been in the forest at night before. I stood there, whispering to myself. "Come on, been in there all the time. Nothing to get you in there."

Still unsure, I reassured myself with. "It's just a light."

I had to know. Clutching the bow, I climbed over the fence, ran across the ride and into the forest.

When I first entered into the trees I was shocked. It was a lot darker than I was used to. The trees and bushes looked different.

They were shapes.

They looked spooky.

The floor of the forest was covered in old, brown pine needles that gave a soft, cushioned carpet to walk on. Here and there were clumps of ferns. The trees seemed quiet and taller than in the daylight. The slight ground fog seemed to blend everything together in a mixture of white, gray and black. Everything looked like it could be hiding a monster or some bloodthirsty animal.

Strangely, I could sense or feel that there was no danger.

The light had been straight ahead when I had seen it last. There was a clearing in that direction, down where the river made a bend. Looking up I could see stars and the moon as the branches parted in a gentle breeze.

I ran from side to side, hiding behind a tree or a clump of ferns. After about five minutes I could see a light glowing in the trees up ahead.

There was no noise; just this beautiful colored light.

The closer I got, the lower I crouched. Maybe these are poachers?

I had heard about poachers. Had my bow and arrows, no problem. If it was poachers then I could sneak away and get help.

Funny how my fear of everything had disappeared. I was actually feeling a warmth and peacefulness.

The clearing was just ahead. Still thinking of poachers, I crept on my belly behind some ferns. Looking through the fern branches I could see into the clearing.

I know what that is, I thought.

The clearing was not very big. For some reason the river made a bend here and had left this little clearing, which had clumps of ferns growing in it. This was one of my favorite places to play.

On the far side of the clearing, just above the trees was a Hovercraft. It just was really a lot quieter than the other one.

I knew what it was because I had been on one when we went to Ireland. My dad had told me how they blow air out of the bottom and could actually, kind of, fly over the water and ground.

This one was floating over the trees. There was some kind of drawbridge, like the ones used in castles, which came out of the bottom. A bunch of blue and white headlights were shining out of the sides. They lit up the clearing so that the fog could be seen moving around.

I had found the light at last.

Wow. Maybe a secret experiment by a mad scientist? I thought.

It was hard to see very clearly because I was still peaking through the fern branches, but I could make out the shapes well enough. The two people walked slowly down the drawbridge.

I think they had something wrong with them or they were very old. They seemed to shuffle along, like my Granny's friend and he was real old.

They reached the clearing and bent over to look at something. Looking around, one of them seemed to have lost something. He or she, it was hard to see, walked slowly over to a clump of ferns and then stood there looking down at them. Then they turned and walked back to the other. Together they walked off into the forest on the far side of the clearing.

It was actually kind of neat. They had this wagon, that had a shiny box on it, with no wheels or rope that followed after them. It was probably a smaller hovercraft.

There was a movement near the edge of the clearing

and I could make out a small deer. It moved across the clearing and went to the same clump of ferns that the guy had looked at before.

Then, to my amazement, a fox was sneaking through the fog towards the same clump of ferns.

Parting the ferns a little, I could see better.

That's when this kid's hand reached out and started to stroke the back of the fox. That was great, see, I had only been able to watch the foxes I had seen.

They must be Gypsies, I thought.

Someone had told me that they could talk to the wild animals, as well as curse or cure you. They also were supposed to buy children. Least that's what my mom used to say. She always said that one day she would sell me to them if I weren't good.

That sense and feeling that nothing was wrong was stronger than ever.

I wondered if that kid could teach me how to touch a fox. Only way to find out was to ask.

Slowly I stood up and started walking through the fog to the clump of ferns. I was almost there when the kid stuck out his head and looked at me.

His head came out so quickly that he caught me off guard. I just stopped real quick and threw up my hand. A big smile coming to my face. He had just scared the living daylights out of me.

"Hi," I said just as quickly.

He just looked at me and slowly tilted his head to one side. I think that his mouth was too small to talk, because he didn't say anything. He just looked at me.

His eyes were very big and black. His nose was really short and the end seemed to missing, because I could see into his nostrils, like a pig's, kind of. He had a big, bald head and someone or something had pulled his ears off.

"Hi," I tried again.

This time he stood up. He wasn't much taller than me. His body reminded me of my sister's dolls. The arms and legs were too big for the body. When he walked it was like a doll too, slowly, stiffly like he was going to fall over. Like he wasn't used to walking.

He was calling me over closer by waving, what was left of his hand, in my direction.

Poor kid. He must have been in some kind of accident because he only had two fingers and what looked like another finger for his thumb. Thick fingers though.

Then I knew that they were Gypsies, because who else would let their kid out to play naked, and he was a weird blue-gray color. Could he be a vampire?

The fox was rubbing against my leg now. Then it rolled over, just like a dog. The other kid reached down and stroked its belly, while the deer started to nuzzle the back if the kid's head. I was starting to think that I wanted my mom to sell me.

"How did you do that?" I asked.

I got the feeling that in order to be this close and to have the animals trust you, you must be very relaxed and calm. The animals must not have any sense of danger from you. You must project peaceful thoughts from your mind to the minds of the creatures.

Then wait until they come to you. Maintain the thoughts

while you comfort them by stroking. They will then stay and play or keep you company.

"Thanks." I was stoking the fox as I answered. I didn't realize that he had not spoken a word because I was paying attention to a real live fox.

"Are you Gypsies?" I asked, wondering if they had a home or if they lived in the hovercraft and just traveled around seeing stuff.

He didn't say anything, but I got the feeling that they were Gypsies. Their home was very, very far away. Probably north past Scotland, because I got the feeling that they were from up there somewhere and they were traveling great distances to see strange and wonderful things.

They had plants and creatures where they came from, once. Things were different at their home now. All the plants and creatures had been destroyed a long time ago. The people did not look after the place where they lived and many bad things had happened, then all was gone. Just the place where they lived was left.

They had different homes too, they were kind of like bubbles, but you could not play outside anymore.

People everywhere had to stop being so selfish and start-paying attention to looking after our forests, rivers and seas or the same thing would happen to us.

"We are. That's what we have the Forest Rangers and the Game Warden for. That's their job."

I think that he was smiling then because he got this soft look to his face and the corner of his eyes narrowed back like mine did when I smiled. It was strange his mouth didn't move though, and for the first time I realized that he was not speaking to me.

"Hey, how do you speak without making any noise?" I asked quickly. Then before he could answer, I added quickly. "Teach me how?"

He slowly shook his head and I whined, "PLEASE."

I was starting to understand that it was not something that could be taught until your brain developed more. There was a lot more that the brain could do, but the thought process had to be cleared of all primal instincts. It required clear, purposeful thoughts directed with a specific intent towards somebody else's brain which could receive it. They in turn would be able to direct their thoughts to you.

There was more that could be done but it would all take time. It was not the right time yet, later he would teach me. I understood that I could receive but not send it back, yet. I was going to practice.

He was stroking the deer's nose.

"Do you play here a lot?"

He was in complete awe of the fox and the deer. I was getting the feeling that he loved the forest as much as I did. That this was like a garden to him. This was a place that he could touch and see things that were no more where he lived.

They went different places all the time but this was their favorite as it reminded them of the beautiful place that had been their home so long ago.

There were not many places as beautiful as this. There were lots of places but none had the colors and life like this. This was considered among a great many Gypsies to be the most special place. It was like a dream.

That was why it was so important for everybody to understand. They were here to help, but we keep ignoring them and hurt them if we caught them. How could they make us understand?

"Well that's your problem. Everybody is scared of Gypsies." I could understand. "Somehow you got to make more friends. Then everything will be all right."

I got the feeling we were friends now. One day he would be able to come back and we would play in the daytime. But, right now I had to go. The others were coming back and they might not understand.

I knew that I should not worry about the forest or the river or the animals. There are too many Gypsies watching to make sure that all would be safe. We were all they had left to remind them of their home and they were not going to let the same thing happen here that happened so far away.

They loved it as much as we did. If we didn't learn in time, the Gypsies were going to come out in the daytime to help, they would help us to understand, but it would be better if we did it on our own.

The others were almost back to the clearing.

I turned and ran back to my hiding spot. Watching, through the fern, I saw his parents come out of the trees. One walked up the drawbridge and the hovering wagon followed into the big, quiet hovercraft.

The other walked over to my new friend. They looked at each other and then, I think it must have been the mom, looked in the direction of the ferns that I was hiding behind.

Her eyes narrowed back and she got that soft look on her face. Deep inside me I knew that everything was all right and as long as the Gypsies were around that it always would be. She stroked the belly of the fox and then the neck of the deer.

They both walked up the drawbridge and inside. The drawbridge was raised and I watched as the hovercraft rose above the trees. Then it changed in to a really fast plane and left, straight up and off to the right a bit.

One day I was going to get me a hovercraft. I felt a little sad now that the kid was gone, but he said he'd come back.

I ran all the way home and got back in to bed. Lying there, I was too excited to sleep. I had to tell my dad.

Quick as I could I got out of bed, ran down the veranda and burst in to my parents' bedroom. My dad just about had a heart attack as I ran in to the room.

"What's the matter?" he croaked.

"Nothing, everything is fine. Guess what?" Then I told my mom and dad the story about the Gypsies in the forest. They sat and listened while I excitedly babbled on.

When I was done my mom said, "What a wonderful dream."

I was confused. "That was no dream."

She pulled me down on the bed between them and wrapped her arms around me as I lay down. "Sometimes," she told me, "a dream can seem very real, but it is still a dream."

"But…"

"No buts. It was a wonderful dream. We all have dreams

that seem real. Some are just like yours. Others about flying in space and things like that. It's time for bed, now go to sleep."

I fell asleep wondering about the dream, or was it real?

No, it must have been a dream, because my mom said so.

A Day of Secrets

Breakfast was good that morning. My granny had made bacon and eggs with a pile of toast. I sat at the table eating, trying to plan my day.

It was hard to plan anything because of the rain. It was one of those English drizzle days. That means it's just wet enough to stop you from going outside to play but dry enough to be constantly told to, "go outside and play."

The food was going down in an absentminded fashion, as I stared out the window down the garden. Granny came and sat at the table.

"Granny, there's nothing to do."

"Well you could go for a walk," she responded. "There's always something to do. You just have to find it."

"Everyone's gone. I'd have to go by myself."

"God puts all kinds of things in the world for little boys to discover. Go find one, have some fun."

I decided that Granny was right. Just 'cause it was a drizzly day and there was nobody around didn't mean I had to have a boring day. She was right. I was going to find out what God had for me today.

Finishing up my breakfast, I pulled on my rubber boots and informed Granny I was off. The drizzle was very fine and I thought the best thing to do was to pay a visit on Chris.

Chris worked on the farm above us and would usually let me ride the tractor beside him. I could hear the tractor in the barn as I walked up the driveway. Chris was already busy.

Making my way to the barn I got sidetracked by the big manure pond.

You see, the farmer would bring his cows in at night. In the morning he would milk them before turning them out in the field. Once the cows were outside, the barn floor would be cleaned. The tractor had a scraper blade on it and would scrape the night's manure down into this big pit at the end of the barn. The pit was shaped like a big swimming pool and held the manure before it was spread on the fields. The spreading was done with the big sprinkler system. You just flipped a switch and presto, the manure was spread out in the field of choice.

It is amazing what will fascinate a seven-year-old.

I was standing under the overhang of the barn roof, out of the drizzle, a collection of small rocks in a neat pile beside me.

The rocks did not sink in the watery-looking manure. Amazing! I was busy creating beautiful stone and manure patterns and considered myself a true artist.

If I could just get one rock in that one spot, it would look like a man. I could hear the tractor, but wasn't paying attention to it. As I bent down and leaned over, for a better rock shot, it happened.

Chris didn't know I was in the barn, and when the scraper blade hit me, I was launched in to the air, over my rock pattern landing about eight feet from the edge of the manure pit.

I remember spitting manure out of my mouth, stunned at how quickly my game had ended. Chris was yelling for me to stay still and hold my arms out.

Did you know that you can't swim in manure? It just makes the situation worse.

The manure was like quicksand and I was being sucked down. Chris had found a rope and came to my rescue. By now only my face and arms were above the surface.

My face turned up to the sky kept the manure out of my mouth mostly. Chris tossed the rope over my face and I grabbed hold of it.

He was laughing, almost uncontrollably, as he hauled me out. "You best go see your Gran."

I didn't say anything. Turning I started home, the crying started as my bewilderment was quickly replaced by fear. This could get me in trouble. Crying, stunned, afraid, covered in manure from head to toe, I made my way home. It was an unpleasant walk as the squishy manure had filled my rubber boots.

I stood outside the back window of the kitchen and yelled. "Granny, help."

She stuck her head out the window. "What?"

I can only imagine what went through her mind as she saw her young grandson standing in the drizzle, covered in manure, crying.

She didn't laugh; she just came out and took me over to the hose. After she had hosed off all the manure, she stripped off my clothes and then wrapped me in a towel. She got my clean clothes, made me a warm drink and sat me by the oven.

"Boy, you can get yourself in a mess." Now she smiled at me.

Realizing that she wasn't upset with me I started to smile too.

Then Granny had an idea. "Why don't you ride your bike in the puddles for a bit?"

"That's a great idea." My drink was finished and being warmed up, I was ready.

Now, my bike was the best in the world. My dad was going to take the training wheels off but had not got around to it yet. My bike was red and had big wide, white tires on it. It could go really fast, and because the training wheels were still on, it could really corner, even if you didn't have much balance.

I rode the bike round our big circular drive once, twice. Then I got bored. The gate was still open, so I rode up to the farmyard.

The farmer's son and I used to ride our bikes through the silage pit all the time.

This pit was a big pit that had dirt piled up all around it. The farmer would cut grass in the fields and put it in the pit, the grass would have some white chemical powder spread on it, and then more grass was put on. The tractor, with a big roller attached, would drive over the grass and press it down. Then the process would be repeated. This and hay was the cow's food in the winter.

This being spring, the pit was almost empty. However, the rain had left this puddle of silage juice, which had an awful, sweet, tangy smell to it.

This looked like a great puddle to ride across. I rode my bike to the top of the hill that led down in to the pit, and parked it there. I was not going to be stupid (my dad always said that I had above average intelligence).

I walked down into the pit and waded out into the puddle to check the depth. Perfect, not quite up to the top of my boots. Back I went to the bike, this was going to be fun. It was also something that I was not supposed to do, 'cause the juice stained your clothes. No sweat, one run and I'm out of here.

I aimed the bike for the middle of the puddle, then started pedaling with a loud whoop. The speed was great. I was flying. Down the hill I went. As the front wheel entered the puddle of brown, smelly juice, I lifted my legs up on the center bar.

Juice was sprayed out to the sides as the wide tires cut a path.

That's when I hit something under the surface.

All I remember was a jerk, thinking "Oh, oh," and a splash.

Then I was sitting in the juice with the bike on its side beside me, one of the training wheels bent backwards. This was not good. Twice in one day, the crying started again. This time I would be in trouble. Picking the bike up, I pushed it home.

Another unpleasant walk home, dread had settled in and the silage juice had filled up my boots, making for another squishy walk.

Standing outside the back window of the kitchen, I yelled, "Granny, help."

She stuck her head out the window. "What?"

The look on her face said it all. There was her special grandson covered in brown juice and stinking to high heaven, again.

"Please don't tell," I begged.

Out she came, over to the hose again, off came the clothes. Here comes the warm drink, fresh clothes and the warm oven.

She asked me if I wanted some lunch, and as she made the sandwich, she said, "You're not having much luck today are you?"

"You told me to ride my bike in the puddles," I accused her.

"Not that one." She sighed in exasperation. Then she added softly. "I won't tell if you don't."

"Deal." I loved Granny; she was always trying to help me out of trouble.

I was sitting there feeling sorry for myself, the sandwich almost finished, when Granny had another idea. "Why don't you go over to Scott's for the afternoon?"

Now that was a good idea. "Okay."

It was a long walk to Scott's. I had to cross three of the farm fields and then go through part of the forest to get there.

My imagination was picturing God up in Heaven laughing. It didn't seem right for him to pick on little boys and where was His big discovery for me?

We had a grand time playing until his little brothers tried to play with us. Soon I was walking home in trouble again. His mom said she was going to call our house. It was something to do with us being in a tree fort, some rocks, the effects of gravity and a bump on the head of Scott's little brother. (Maybe another time you can ask.)

I was about halfway across the last field before our property, wondering how much trouble I was in and what was gravity anyway?

How was I supposed to know what would happen?

Probably going to get a good spanking this time. This was not turning out to be a good day.

Probably get sent to bed without dinner too.

I was just too dejected to cry. So I just shuffled home, head hanging down, hands in my pockets.

That was when I learned that there are just some things in life that you can not escape.

I cocked my head to the side, that was a sound I knew, but what was it again? I looked around. The sound was all around me. Kind of like a loud whooshing of air.

The words escaped my mouth at the same time I remembered what the sound was.

"Oh no, not again."

That same instant, my worst fear came true. I watched as the manure sprinklers came on. The sound had been the air being pushed out of the pipes as the smelly stuff made its way out to the sprinkler heads. It was now being spread all around me. All over me. The whole field was being covered. It was shooting out of the big sprinkler heads in big dripping arcs. Not one inch of ground was left uncovered. Not one inch of me was left uncovered.

There was no escape.

Dejectedly, I walked on, trying my best to avoid the

main spray. It did no good. There was no use running. I wiped it off my head and face and walked home.

Standing outside the back window of the kitchen, I yelled, "Granny, help!"

She stuck her head out the window. "What?"

This time she laughed softly. There stood her grandson, her wonderful grandson covered in brown, smelly manure again. She came out and got the hose. She hosed me off, stripped me off, got clean clothes, got the warm drink and sat me by the oven.

"You're not having a good day," she stated.

"No kidding and it's going to get worse."

"Oh, you mean Scott's brother?"

"Did his mom call?"

"Yes."

"Does my mom know?"

"No, she is still out."

"She's going to be real mad when she finds out."

"Well, I think that you've been punished enough for one day, so I don't think she needs to find out."

"Thanks Granny. This has been the worst day."

I was playing in my room when my dad came in from work.

"I'm going for a walk. Want to come?"

"No thanks."

He tried again. "You could ride your bike."

"No thanks, I think I'll just play in my room. Been a bad day."

I know he was trying to figure out what exactly was wrong with me. Granny had been great and was now busy doing laundry, lots of laundry. Nobody knew anything about what had happened that day. It was a secret between my Granny and me.

"Hey Dad, what's gravity?" I asked him.

Looking very perplexed he said, "Maybe I'll stay and play with you for a while."

Thinking about the day, the secrets I had and the look on his face, that was probably a good idea. It had been a trying day, but maybe it could still be salvaged.

When I said my prayers that night I remembered to thank God for Granny. She was one of those things that God put in the world for little boys to discover.

Meet Mademoiselle

"Next time we should tie an anchor to a tree."

"Hmm…that might work, but it's still gonna sink," he replied.

It was a warm, sunny day as we walked down the long driveway towards my house. Michael and I had been rafting down in the swamp-pond between his barn and the river, without any luck. He had already changed at his place and now was coming to our place for the first time.

It was uncommon for me to bring someone home, but since nobody was there and we wouldn't be long, I thought it would be safe. What could happen in the time it would take me to change?

The gravel crunched under our feet as we walked down the long driveway, with the spring daffodils in full bloom on either side. A smile crept over my face as my mood relaxed and I wondered what Michael would think of our home.

The thought crossed my mind about warning him of my parent's love for animals.

"Come on in. I'll be quick, then we can go do something else."

I had not known him very long, as we had only moved into the house about a month before. His dad was Farmer Day and he owned the last farm that you have to cross to get to Carpenter's. Both of our parents were very glad that we were about the same age as no other kids lived on Two-Mile Lane. In the future they would come to regret the day we met. But for now, we were encouraged to play together.

"What's that?" asked Michael as we opened the door of my bedroom.

"That's my mom's dog, Tasha. Don't worry about her. She used to belong to a puppy farmer who beat her with a chain. Broke her ribs and her nose with it. She don't smell very well now."

Tasha was a beautiful blonde Afghan. She was laying almost the full length of the bed and was holding her elegant head in the air to get a better look at Michael.

"Just say hello softly and she'll go back to sleep," I told him.

In a soft voice Michael said, "Hi Tasha."

She put her ears back and looked at him with her soft eyes, sneezed, thumped her tail twice and went back to sleep. She knew she was safe.

Another sneeze.

This one was from the other side of the open door that led to the next bedroom. All the rooms had adjoining doors so in bad weather we didn't have to use the veranda to get from one area of the house to another. Soda had been sleeping in one of the bedrooms; we must have woken him up.

Soda walked headfirst into the doorframe, backed up one step, turned towards us and sneezed again. His six-inch beard was wrapped around his nose and his eyes, blinding him.

Michael had the most astonished look on his face. "What the..." he whispered.

"That's Soda, my dad's Schnauzer. He's old and almost blind. When his beard does that it tickles his nose."

Soda sneezed again, as if on cue.

I walked over and rescued him from his beard by using my fingers to comb it down. His senses now free, he realized Michael was at the door and growled lowly. I could feel his chest rumble as I held him.

"Michael, come over here and hold out your hand so he can smell you, then he'll be fine."

Doing as I asked, he came over and held out his hand, Soda sniffed it and stopped his display of macho dog protector.

Michael laughed. "He don't look like he could do much."

I laughed back. "If he can find you he'll bite. If he does anything, stay about four feet away and he can't see you."

As Michael sat in the chair under the front window, Soda started to move forward. Watching Soda out of the corner of my eye, I changed out of my dirty, wet clothes. Michael's eyes got bigger as Soda slowly made his way forward. A smile came over his face as we watched him.

Soda walked forward slowly. His nose sniffing first in Michael's direction and then mine. He could smell our presence but we were just out of eyesight. As he swung his head back towards Michael, he took another step and went headfirst into the table beside the chair.

Surprising himself he jumped back one step, turned left, walked across the bedroom and went head first in to the bed.

Tasha opened her eyes, lifted her elegant head, and then looking down her long nose, saw who it was and went back to sleep.

Soda backed up one step, made a right turn and was headed straight for the fireplace. His left front paw stepped on the hearthrug, stopping; he lowered his head, and made sure this was the place he wanted, then lay down. There was a big sigh as he put his head down.

Michael looked at me. "That's really sad."

"No," I replied, "the sad part is until we put the rug there, he used to bang his head on the fireplace grate, back up and have to make another left to go sleep under the other window."

We both started to laugh.

As I was about to start explaining how my mother loved animals, even ones that others might put to sleep, Soda interrupted again. There was another very loud sigh and then he produced a rather loud, rude noise.

Looking at him in surprise and then at each other, we burst out laughing. "Sorry, he doesn't have any manners." I told Michael.

His laughing stopped as his face contorted in revulsion, while he started waving his hand in front of his face.

Laughing even harder I added, "Stinks too."

"Thanks for the warning," he said from behind the waving hand. "Anything else you need to warn me about."

I looked at Mademoiselle. She was sleeping on the floor, the sun keeping her warm. Should I tell him about her?

"Well," I started, "if that cat wakes up, you might want

to sit still."

"Why?" he asked as he looked at the small, brown cat sleeping.

"She's just a little different, but as long as she stays asleep nothing will happen," I replied.

I had a clean sweater stuck on the top of my head as I heard him say, "The cat's waking up."

Pulling the sweater down with a yank, I half-whispered, "Let's go, quick."

"Why?" he asked.

"Because she woke up."

"So?"

I really didn't feel like explaining about Mademoiselle. Then, looking at the expression on Michael's face, I realized he wasn't going anywhere without an explanation.

"Alright," I said with a sigh, "come on. I'll introduce you to her, but you remember this was your idea."

Mademoiselle was a perfect Burmese cat. She had a deep chocolate brown coat, short hair and big beautiful yellow-gold eyes. Her coat had been sunburned a little, which gave it a red sheen that sparkled in the sun. She was two years old and weighed about five pounds. Her face was round with a slightly elongated nose, ears that sat perfectly on her head; she was the perfect show cat.

Except for a few very obvious faults.

So far she was still lying in a ball on the floor, however her eyes were now open.

"Her name is Mademoiselle."

He made a sucking noise with his mouth. "Here kitty, kitty."

"She's stone deaf, Michael."

He looked at me. "What?"

A perverse smile crept over my face. I always took great pleasure in watching people's faces as they discovered that this was a most unusual animal.

"She is more than just a deaf cat, you know." Then with a smile firmly imbedded on my face I asked. "You sure you really want to meet her?"

Michael looked at the small brown cat that was lying in a ball, head on the floor and its eyes wide open. A look of confusion crossed his face as he replied. "Sure."

Crossing the room, I sat on the chair by the fireplace.

This was the part I liked best. I had him curious now and expecting something.

"Michael," I announced in a loud voice, Tasha raised her head at the intrusion, and Soda slept on. "Meet Mademoiselle."

Then I stamped my foot on the floor.

The small cat leapt to her feet in an instant.

Michael gasped quietly and without taking his eyes from her, whispered, "You broke it."

I was watching his reaction and laughing uncontrollably. I loved that reaction to her.

Mademoiselle stood in the exact spot that she had been sleeping in. Her tail, sticking up in the air, had a ninety-degree kink in it; about two inches from the tip that went to the right. Her feet were spread out from her body and you could tell from the way that her muscles were twitching, that she was ready to take flight but could not figure out the correct direction yet.

47

It was her head that gave away the fact that this was not a normal cat. It always moved like one of those dogs that people put in the back window of their cars. No matter what she did, her head bobbed up and down in a circular motion and always in a direction that was about one inch left of center.

As a result she had a tendency to look like she was going one way, when she was really going another.

She made quite the first impression, but I knew the best was yet to come.

Tasha was now paying attention to the cat. She knew better than to go after her and also knew not to take her eyes of her. Soda still slept.

"Does it move?" Michael asked.

"Sure," I replied and waved my hand near the floor to get her attention.

Her eyes fixed on my hand as her head bobbed around, making her look like one of those clown dolls whose eyes would roll around. After about thirty seconds of watching my hand she decided to come over.

As Michael watched her walk to me his eyes got wider yet and my smile got bigger. It took everything I had not to burst out laughing, but I knew the show was just beginning.

She gathered her feet beneath her and the adventure started. She kept her eyes fixed on my hand so she knew where to end up and started to walk, head bobbing around, eyes fixed straight ahead.

It looked like her head rotated around her eyeballs.

Unfortunately, she could not walk in a straight line. It

was more like a series of circles that were connected together, so as you watched her go from point A to point B you were reminded of a very stretched out Slinky. There was nothing wrong with her back legs, but she always lifted her back right paw so quickly that it thrust one of her hips above her back making her wobble and look like she was going to fall over.

Halfway across the room I said, "Watch this," and lifted my hand from her field of vision.

She stopped in mid-step, head bobbing. I put my hand back and she continued her wobbly, bobbing, spiraling motion towards me.

Michael muttered, "What the?" as he was fascinated by our little brown cat.

"Wait. Watch this," I said as Mademoiselle approached my chair.

She was within reach, so I put my hand on her head and ran it down her back. Sitting back in the chair I waited for the next move, which I knew would be a jump onto my lap. The stroke of her back always made her want more.

She stood at my feet bobbing her head and I knew that she was trying to work out distances, speeds, landing points, angles and whatever else went through a cat's mind before it jumped.

Then with her eyes locked on to my lap, her head bobbing up, down and around, she turned her body ninety degrees to the chair and leaped.

Michael gasped, as she appeared to be jumping at him. Then almost at the top of her jump into thin air, she jerked her back legs around she that she changed direction and

49

landed with a thump on my lap.

I grimaced slightly as her nails went through my jeans and she got her balance. Once her world stopped spinning and she had her balance, she retracted her nails from my legs and bobbed her circling head in my direction as if to apologize. Her pupils were the full size of her eyes after her wild flight, but she almost had a smile on her face as though she was proud of her wonderful landing.

Settling herself on my knees, her back towards me, sitting upright, surveying the room with her bobbing and weaving head, she started to purr as I stroked her back.

Michael raised his eyebrows as the sound reached him; even this was unusually loud, harsh and, well, almost broken.

I noticed that he was just staring at her, shaking his head in amazement.

Forcing the smile from my face I dead-panned, "You should her eat!"

We both started to howl with laughter at the same time.

Tasha watched Mademoiselle from the bed and then a very bad odor wafted across the room from Soda's direction.

Still laughing and gasping for air, Michael was almost crying as he said, "Open the window."

"Can you open it? If I move Mademoiselle she'll try and jump on you."

Michael got up and opened the window. Tasha got up off the bed and followed him. The whole time she watched the crazy cat sitting, bobbing its head.

"Hey, could you let her out too? She knows what this

cat is like. Thanks."

With the dog outside and the breeze coming in from the window, he returned to his chair.

"Now," he started, "what's with the cat."

It was time to let the joke go and tell him about our bobbing, weaving, deaf, kinky-tailed and spastic miracle cat.

"Well, she had an accident when she was about five or six days old."

He got a serious look on his face that seemed to get more intense as I continued. "I watched it happen, scared the dickens out of me. There was nothing I could do; it happened so fast. The mother was on the floor feeding all the kittens and all of a sudden she jumped up to a shelf that was about four feet high. She moved so fast that one of the kittens stayed attached to her teat. When she landed on the shelf the kitten hit the edge and was knocked loose. It fell to the floor and landed on its head and broke its neck."

Shaking his head in disbelief he added. "And lived!"

"Yup. My mom saved her. She has kind of a big bust and she just picked it up and popped it between her boobs. She carried it around like that for weeks. Everywhere she went the kitten went with her. She hand fed it and kept it warm. Then when it was old enough she used to let it wobble around. By then it was too late to put her down cause we all liked it. We didn't find out it was deaf until later and we didn't realize how brain damaged she was until she got older. We just let her in with rest of the cats and she learned stuff from them, I guess."

"Wow." He was in total awe. I don't know if he had ever seen anything like this before.

"She really is healthy," I continued. "She just has a few problems but other than that she is fine."

I paused for a moment, thinking that I should warn him, just in case. "She has one problem that I need to warn you about."

He stopped watching her bobbing head and focused on me. "What exactly is that?" he asked, trying hard not to laugh anymore.

Playing up the moment, I answered. "Umm, she kind of has these fits every once in a while."

"What kind of fits?" he questioned without smiling.

"Well, it's like she gets real excited all of a sudden, and then she kind of goes really fast all over the place. The worst part is you can never be quite sure where she is going and we are not sure that she knows either."

He looked like he was going to start laughing again, so I continued quickly.

"If you see her start running around, watch her. She may came at you but don't move 'cause she will probably change direction."

"And if she doesn't?" he asked

"Cover your privates," we both said together.

The last part cracked us both up again. "Are you serious?" he croaked.

"Yup. Want to see her eat? Now that's amazing."

We carried Mademoiselle through the open doorway into the next bedroom. Crossing that room to another door, which led into the animal kitchen. Her food was waiting for her and I put her down in front of it.

Michael's face was getting this look of concern and disbelief again. It was like every time something new happened here, his eyes had to check with his brain to make sure nothing was disconnected.

He was looking at the setup on the floor.

The plate of food was on the floor and beside it there was about four feet of newspaper spread out to the left of the plate. He got a puzzled look of anticipation on his face as Mademoiselle approached the food.

She stepped forward to the plate, then, doing the bob-weave-circle thing, she took a sniff. She kind of cycled her head around so she looked at me, then the food, then Michael, back to the food, me again, stopped over the food and dropped her open mouth into it. Closing her mouth, she had a hold of the food.

As she brought her head up, she twisted it sideways quickly and opened her mouth. This resulted in the food flying out of her mouth, which she proceeded to chase with her teeth snapping at it.

Michael was stunned.

He just stood watching as sometimes the food would get eaten but mostly, it flew about three feet and landed with a thwack on the paper while she seemed to lose sight of it, snap her teeth in thin air, pause in wonder, then bob back over the plate to start the process again.

"That is so cool," was all he could manage this time.

"We should get going," I reminded him.

"Wait a minute, I want to see this."

He had no idea. "That's going to take her about an hour

to eat," I prompted.

"I want to see one of those fits," he said as he looked at me and started laughing again.

"If I show you a fit, can we go?"

He was nodding his head. "Yeah."

Picking her up, we headed back to my bedroom. This we needed a little space for.

Sitting back down, I held Mademoiselle on my lap and instructed Michael to stand behind the chair that he had been sitting in earlier.

"You won't hurt her will you?" He was suddenly concerned about her.

"No, of course not."

I put my hands on her sides and rubbed them back and forth on her coat, very fast for about ten seconds. When I stopped she sat straight up and bobbed her head a few times. I knew when it was going to happen before Michael, as her claws slowly worked their way in to my legs again.

Then it happened.

She launched herself in a curvy, flying arc off my lap.

She did the back twist and landed with her legs spread apart, her claws digging in to the carpet as she landed.

She stood doing the bob and weave, maybe to make sure that the Earth was not rotating too fast.

Then she snapped her head to the left, spiral ran about four feet, dug her front claws into the carpet, snap twisted her back around, and took off, spiraling, across the room.

She reached the other side and repeated the snap twist move again, this time, along the floor at the end of my bed.

She arrived at my little sister's dollhouse (which I had been using as a base for my soldiers) in the blink of an eye.

Hitting her head on the dollhouse, she sprang into the air and landed on the hearthrug, almost on top of Soda.

Poor Soda, he woke up with a start and looked at her. She was standing in the typical landing position; legs spread, claws dug in. Soda's fright was obvious by the return of the bad odor.

She just stood there looking straight at him. Her head bobbing in a circle, waiting.

Soda put his head down with a sigh and went back to sleep; he was too old for this.

Mademoiselle curled up against his belly and put her head down; eyes wide open.

Laughing and with Michael shaking his head, we let Tasha back in. She looked at the two on the rug, jumped on the bed, stretched out, yawned and put her head down.

As Michael and I went in search of other things to do, I wondered what he would do when he met my dog Charlie.

The rest of the week at school, I listened as Michael recounted the vision he had seen.

As I listened to him tell the story, I knew he had seen the miracle too. He had fallen under her spell of love.

It's funny how we all seem to miss the miracles that happen in front of us every day. I guess we are just too busy now.

Why I Like Omelettes

"Murderer," my mother said with a cracking voice. Turning quickly on her heel, she almost pulled Johanna off her feet as she made for the car.

Dad had a blank look on his face as he watched her drive away through the gate to Carpenter's.

He sighed quietly and I could sense the exasperation he felt.

I understood the situation. Full of anxiety, I was also curious about what was to take place. Dad had decided that I was old enough to learn that death was a part of life, people ate meat and what that meant.

"Wait here," he said, without looking at me.

My parents had to work all the time to support us when we were young. They cut corners where they could and it still wasn't enough. Dad came up with the brilliant idea of raising our own turkeys.

Now where as this was a good idea, it was not such a good idea for a family that loved animals. We got the chicks young and hand fed them. They ran around our property with some of our dogs and formed quite a formidable pack.

More than a few visitors where surprised when they got out of their cars and had their vision tested, as a pack of barking, gobbling, fur and feathers came charging around the corner of the house to repel the intruders.

Johanna and I used to hide and laugh as they jumped

back in their cars.

Sometimes hikers would walk down the lane and venture past the barn towards the forest. The turkeys sitting under the bushes would be surprised by the hikers, and suddenly start flapping their wings and squawk-gobbled at them. Some ran into the barn for protection, only to be chased back out by Granny's very grumpy goat, Nanny. Others broke into a sprint for the forest gate and still others tripped over backwards, landing on their rear ends in a mud-puddle, with a look of shock on their face.

It was all great fun.

Unfortunately for him, Bert had grown to be the plumpest bird first.

Dad had locked the rest of the animals away, nobody else should get hurt.

I thought that was very thoughtful of him. I wouldn't want to watch my friend get killed either.

Mom started to get upset as the finality of the situation set in. She liked Bert. We all did. He was Bert. He was also Sunday dinner.

She had pleaded in vain for his life, then had decided to take Johanna out for a drive.

Dad came back with his shotgun, then called Bert, "Here turkey, turkey."

When we fed them, we always called them like that. Bert was poking around in the garden when he heard the call. His head popped up and he came at the run.

"Gobble, Gobble." Had to be first.

"Gobble." Got to be first.

"Gobble, Gobble, Gobble." Need food.

Raising the gun to his shoulder my father took aim at the approaching bird.

I stuck my fingers in my ears and scrunched up my face, anticipating the impending blast.

Peeking through squinting eyes. I wanted to look, without seeing.

"Gobble." Bert had arrived and was searching for the grain that should be here.

Click.

"Gobble, Gobble." Bert was still searching.

The first hammer had fallen into place without producing a blast from the gun.

"What the…" my father whispered.

Click.

The second hammer fell into place with the same silent result.

"Gobble." Bert cocked his head to one side as his beady bird eyes questioned us for his food.

Dad quickly broke the shotgun open. A smile crossed his face as he realized that my mother had removed the shells that he had loaded earlier.

"Something wrong?" I asked.

"No. Be right back."

Bert was halfway back to the garden, when Dad came back. "Here turkey, turkey."

The still hungry bird swung his head around, the body followed and Bert was on a collision course with destiny. With my fingers replaced in my ears and looking through scrunched up eyes again, I watched as the shotgun was put to Dad's shoulder and Bert approached.

"Gobble, Gobble."

He had no idea what was about to happen and as a result had no fear.

My father stood and took aim.

"Gobble."

Bert got closer.

"Gobble, Gobble."

And closer.

"Gobble."

I watched as Bert started to look for food by pecking inside the barrel.

Not finding anything to eat, he looked over the barrel at my father.

"Gobble, gobble." You could hear the confusion in his call. There was supposed to be food here.

There was food here all right, just not for him.

My father uttered, "Damn, I'll get too much shot in him. Got to do it another way." Part of me suspected that was a lie. I think he liked Bert too.

Opening my eyes and removing my fingers, my smart mouth now speaking. "What now, Big White Hunter?"

My father laughed. "Caveman style." He put the gun down against the veranda, then strode across the yard to a pile of wood.

Bert was now searching the area around the steps in search of the elusive food, while I sat on the step to watch.

My father picked up a two by four that was about four feet long, then came and sat on the steps with me.

"What are you going to do with that?" I asked.

He looked at me. "I'm going to whack him in the back

of the head."

"Gobble." Bert was standing in front of us. Occasionally he pecked at the ground, but mostly he just waited for food. My father started talking to him.

"You know if you would turn around we could get this over with." Bert gobbled at him.

"Can't talk your way out of this, turn around." Bert gobbled again, pecked at the ground, and looked at me, then my dad.

"Gobble."

"Maybe if we ignore him, he'll turn around, then POW," my father said. We pretended to talk to each other.

Looking back, I think it must have been hard for him. Why else would he be sitting there, talking mumbo jumbo with his young son, while trying to out psyche a turkey. I was sure he knew what he was doing, he was my father. So we made noises at each other and waited for Bert to turn.

Then it happened. Bert must have gotten tired of waiting for grain and turned.

"Finally." My father was watching as his quarry was returning to the vegetable patch. He let Bert get about ten feet away and then slowly got up to pursue him.

Bert had found something of interest in the grass and stopped to investigate. My father grasped the plank with both hands and raised it above his shoulder. Slowly and quietly, he closed the distance. He was right behind our future meal as Bert raised his head from the grass. I heard my father draw in a full breath and prepared myself for the blow.

"Gobble, Gobble." Bert had spun his head around and was looking at Dad again. One eye blinking, then the other.

"Gobble."

My father standing frozen in time, reminded me of the Statue of Liberty attempting murder.

"Gobble." That one had a questioning tone in it.

"Damn. Turn around again."

Lowering the board, my father had an exasperating tone in his voice. "Stupid bird."

As he started to back away, Bert turned to continue to the garden. My father's reflexes kicked in as he saw his chance. He took a step forward, swinging the board like a baseball bat at the back of Bert's head.

WHACK.

There was a horrible sound as it thudded against the bird's skull. My father followed through the swing and looked back at his victim. The disbelief in his eyes as Bert looked back, had me roaring with laughter.

Bert cocked his head to one side, blinked at him and with a "Gobble, gobble," continued on to the garden.

"Strike One!" I yelled.

"You be quiet," my father retorted.

He was now storming after Bert. The board was raised; Bert didn't see him coming.

Dad swung again, just as Bert found something in the grass. As his head went down the two by four grazed his comb. The ineffectual blow spun my father off balance. Spinning all the way around, his eyes met Bert's blinking gaze again.

"Gobble, gobble."

"Strike two!" I yelled.

Now my father started to chase Bert, like a man possessed. He was running around, swinging at him, telling him to stand still and take it like a man.

"OY. What the bleed'in hell are you doin'?"

Turning to the front gate we both saw Alf coming towards us.

He was our coal-man and had been riding his bike to the house to check if we needed any coal for the fireplaces. He was dressed all in black and still covered, head to toe, with coal dust.

Leaning with his arms on the top of the handlebars, he removed his cap with one hand and was rubbing his head.

"Alf?" my father said in surprise. He lowered his weapon and ventured over to talk about the afternoon happenings.

"I've got to kill this bird for Sunday dinner."

"That's not how you kill a turkey," Alf commentated. "I was watching you chase that bleedin' bird."

"Well, how would you do it then?" questioned my dad.

"Bring him over there and slam his head in the gate, best I reckon."

Now, my father being an intelligent man could see how this would work. "Here turkey, turkey."

Bert came running across the yard, again expecting food.

"Right," Alf said, opening the gate, "grab him and put is neck against the post."

Dutifully, my father ushered Bert toward the gate. Holding his body, he managed to steer Bert's head and neck against the gatepost. Alf, standing on the opposite side of the gate, was holding it open with one of his huge arms.

Everybody was in position.

"Ready?" yelled Alf.

"Ready," answered my father.

Using all the strength he had, Alf slammed the gate shut.

The force of it slamming shut made both gate posts vibrate.

I was standing looking at Bert's body, with its head disappearing into the wooden gate frame.

It was done.

Looking over the gate, Dad and Alf looked at Bert's head sticking out the other side. Bert was motionless and his blinking eyes were silently closed.

"That ought do it." Alf smiled. Then turned to retrieve his bike and leave.

My father had a slight look of sadness on his face as he opened the gate.

As the gate opened, Bert stood up, gave his head a shake, blinked at Alf then at my father.

"Gobble, Gobble."

Dad and Alf stared at him. Then determination set in.

"Right," said Alf, as he dropped his bike and walked through the gate. My father had caught hold of Bert, who was still trying to shake the cobwebs out of his head.

"Stick his head back there again," Alf commanded, as he took hold of the situation.

Dad steered a stunned Bert back to the gate. Once his head was through, Alf slammed the gate again. Looking over the gate, they could see Bert's motionless head, eyes closed.

"He's playing dead again, he is," Alf stated.

"What now?" asked my father.

Alf looked at him. "Now, grab a hold of his body and pull hard. That ought to break his neck."

With Alf watching intently, my father grabbed a hold of Bert's body and gave it a sharp, hard yank. Then lowered the body to the ground. Bert's legs folded under the weight of his body.

Alf and my father looked at each other with smiles on their faces. They shook hands on a job well done, and Alf opened the gate so Dad could retrieve our Sunday dinner.

Bert felt the pressure on his neck relax and stood up, shaking his head and blinking at the two men.

"Gobble, gobble."

"Bleed'in hell," they both muttered at the same time.

Alf looked at my father. "You sure that bird's not too tough to eat?" They both started laughing.

"Right," my father took over now, "one more time."

Back went Bert's head in to the gate; Alf slammed the gate again.

This time both men took a hold of Bert.

My father counted it off. "One, two, three, pull."

With both men giving it all they had, they yanked Bert's body away from the gate viciously. Afraid that it was not done yet, they kept pulling for about a minute.

Finally, they placed the body on the ground. Tentatively, they opened the gate. Bert gently slid to the ground. Some tears slowly rolled down my face. Bert was gone.

Alf picked up his bike and turned to my dad.

"That's how you kill a turkey," he said, then mounted his bike.

We watched as Alf peddled off through the farmyard.

When he had gone, my father looked down at me. "Well at least we got dinner. You all right?" he asked.

The tears were slowing now. I looked at him and thought my mother was right, it was murder.

"Yeah," I responded with a sob. It was something that had to be done and I knew that, but I didn't like it.

He reached down to pick up the motionless Bert. As his hands touched Bert's wings, Bert's head suddenly sprung up.

"GOBBLE," he squawked indignantly.

Bert was alive.

We looked at him, then at each other. Laughter burst out from us and my dad sat on the ground in convulsions.

I hugged Bert.

"Gobble, Gobble." He squirmed away and headed back towards the garden.

He was alive.

"Umm...Dad...what do we do now?"

"Don't tell Alf." He chuckled.

"I mean for Sunday dinner."

"Come with me and I'll show you."

He was still chuckling to himself as he led me down to the barn.

As he opened the door, the other two turkeys came out.

"Don't let them get away," he said holding his arms wide and steering them up the driveway towards the gate.

Together we chased them up to Farmer Day's house.

Dad traded the two turkeys for three chickens and two dozen eggs.

"Are chickens easier to kill?" I asked.

"We're not killing the chickens."

"What are we going to do with them?"

"I'm going to show you how to make the greatest omelette in the world."

My mother came home about an hour later. She walked up to my father and handed him the axe. "You might need this."

"That's not how you kill a turkey," he told her. She started to cry softly and my father put his arm around her.

"Gobble." Bert appeared almost out of nowhere.

Mom's eyes lit up at the sight of him.

"Gobble, Gobble."

"How about chickens?" he asked. "You should see what I can do to an omelette."

She threw her arms around him and all was forgiven. I learned the lesson that Dad was trying to teach me.

Death is a part of life, people eat meat and that's why we have supermarkets.

Smoking is Bad

"Dad, can I build a fort?"

My dad was busy putting up new windows on the house. "Sure."

The new windows were going to be great. Carpenter's was an old Victorian house and the old windows let in the cold too much. There was a big fireplace in each room to ward off the winter cold and the dampness. Dad had taught me to light the fire in my room and as long as it wasn't too big, I could have one pretty much whenever I wanted.

"Blasted windows." Dad was getting frustrated with his chore. This was the perfect time for a seven-year-old to ask for anything and I knew it. One thing I had learned from my vast life experience was that timing was everything.

However, first there had to be the obligatory offer of help, which had a ninety-five percent chance of it being accepted. Even if it was accepted, I knew that it would only last about five minutes before the suggestion would be made for me to; "Go play or something."

"Do you want some help?" I asked sweetly.

"No that's alright, this is a one man job. Why don't you go play with Michael?"

Success.

I had the official authority to play with my friend and

to build a fort. Michael was the only person to play with in a three-mile radius of our house, which was surrounded by 1000 acres of forest and 1000 acres of farmland.

My father was still struggling with the windows when Michael and I showed up again. "Dad, can we build a fort out of the old windows?"

He mumbled some words that were unrecognizable as he struggled with removing a window. "Sure."

Michael and I set to work. We hauled the old windows away up the driveway and into one of the horse paddocks. Under a huge, old Chestnut tree, we set to work. The windows were about four feet high and two feet wide. Each one had several smaller panes of glass that were held in place by smaller wooden frames. We stood them up and leaned the tops against each other, in a triangle framework.

It was a great fort. It was three windows long and two leaning at the back closed it off. Michael and I sat in it, very proud of ourselves. We could see all around (in case my sister was coming) and we could talk and plan without *some*one finding out our secret plans. The chairs were made of stumps that we found and we had a big log in front to sit on.

Dad had decided to take a break and came up to see what we were doing. That was when all the trouble started. Now don't take that the wrong way. Dad was really a great guy, but sometimes he gave me ideas that maybe you shouldn't give to a bored, determined and creative young boy.

"Boy, you have done a good job," he said as he sat on the log with a sigh. He had this big grin on his face, like he wanted to stay and play in the fort too.

"Do you really like it?"

"Yes, but something is missing." He looked around for a moment and then came up with a brilliant idea.

"Every fort should have a fire pit." How it had escaped me was a mystery, but my dad didn't miss much.

"You know," he continued, "if you scraped away the dirt over here and built a ring of stones, you could build one. Then tonight, you could have a fire."

Michael and I looked at each other.

Did he really say that? What a great idea!

"Really?" I asked.

Dad was getting up to go back to work. "Sure."

"A real fire?" I questioned in disbelief.

"As long as it's in a contained area and not too big, it will be fine."

"A real fire?"

"I'll check later. As long as you do it right, yes, a real fire."

Michael and I were beaming from ear to ear. Dad went back to work with a big grin on his face. He really did like to teach me new things and felt really good when he could make me happy.

Boy had he done a good job this time.

We set to work and pretty soon had a nice area, in front of the log, cleaned off. Finding some portable stones, we surrounded the pit with two rings and put a third ring on top of those two. That looked like a contained bowl. Then we put sticks in the middle for kindling.

We were ready for fire.

The anticipation was killing us.

Sitting on the log, we surveyed our handiwork. We didn't hear Johanna come up behind us.

"What you doin'?" she asked.

"Getting ready for a fire and you can't come," I replied smugly.

"I'm tellin'."

"No, Dad said."

"I'm tellin' Mom."

The hairs suddenly stood up on the back of my neck. I hadn't thought of Mom. She didn't mind me having fun but she was a mom. That meant that any potential for danger carried a "veto" that would outweigh my dad's "yes".

"Wait!" I cried too late. She was already making a beeline to the house as fast as her short legs would move.

"Now what?" Michael asked.

Thinking for a second, I came up with the answer. "Dad told me that in a situation like this, you pray first, then compromise as much as you can."

We started with the praying.

It didn't take long for my mother to show up with Johanna in tow. Fake tears running down her cute little face.

"Uh, oh," I mumbled as I noticed Mom had a very determined look on her face.

"What is going on?" she demanded.

Michael stared at the fire pit. Mom didn't like him much as we always got into trouble together. We didn't mean to, we just did. I liked Michael but I blamed him for everything to get out of trouble. Which was all right 'cause he always told his mom that it was my fault.

"Nothing," I answered meekly.

"Then why is Johanna crying?"

"I dunno'."

Johanna's tears had stopped now and she was doing a magnificent job of taking deep breaths and heaving her chest. One word came out of her mouth between each breath.

Boy, she was good.

"He..."

"Won't..."

"Let..."

"Me..."

"Come..."

"To..."

"The..."

"Fire..."

Mom looked at me sternly. "What fire?"

"Dad said we could have a fire tonight."

All of a sudden a two-tone yell pierced the air that sounded like my father's name. It started out in a low tone and then changed to a much higher pitch. Thank goodness for piano lessons, otherwise I would not have known the difference between my mother's song and a dead animal.

"G...Lynnnnn."

Michael stuck his fingers in his ears at the volume.

I stuck my elbow in his ribs.

He removed his fingers.

Mom glowered at him.

We looked at the fire pit.

Johanna sobbed.

Dad came at the run, huffing and puffing, as fast as he could.

"What's wrong?"

Mom looked at him questionably. "Fire?"

"Where?" he answered looking around at the house.

"Here."

"Here?"

"Tonight."

"Yes."

"Why?"

"Fort."

"Johanna?"

"Bed." I butted in to the conversation. I should have known better.

"Quiet." They both responded at the same time.

"Johanna?" Mom said.

"Yes."

"Settled."

"Settled."

Johanna stopped sobbing.

Mom left.

Dad went back to his windows.

"See," I said to Michael, "that's how you compromise."

"Praying helped too," he whispered.

We looked at Johanna, who stuck out her tongue and left also.

After supper Johanna, Michael and I sat on the log waiting. The sun was setting behind Carpenter's. All the animals had been fed. The big tree between our property and Day's farm was silhouetted against the clouds forming in the night sky.

Dad showed up, carrying some newspaper and a pail of water. "Well, let's get a fire going."

All three of us cried, "Yeah," at the same time.

"First of all," he started, "we put a ball of paper in the middle of the pit."

Michael and I were paying close attention. Johanna was busy counting her fingers or something like that.

"First a ball of paper," I repeated.

The paper was rolled up and put in middle. "Now we lean some small sticks against the paper to make a little tee-pee."

"Small sticks in a tee-pee."

"Making sure to leave spaces between each stick for air to get in."

"Small spaces for air."

He was busy placing the sticks on. When I had a question.

"Umm, why do we need air?"

"Because," he explained, "air has the oxygen that the fire needs to burn. The oxygen has to be able to get to the bottom of the fire to burn."

"Why?"

"Because that's were the fire starts."

"Why?"

Exasperated he turned to look at me. "Because if it was on the top it would all burn away and there would be no fire."

"The wood's on top and it burns!" Michael input.

"Yes, wood on top, oxygen underneath."

"We want fire!" yelled Johanna.

"How do we light it?" I asked.

Michael had the answer. "Rub two sticks together."

Mine was better. "Flint and stone."

"Matches," Dad said as he produced a pack and handed it to me. He was smart. We needed him.

He looked at me. "Now light a match and hold it to the corner of the paper."

I did as I was told and as the paper burned it set the small sticks on fire.

"Now add some slightly bigger sticks."

We did that and we now had a fire. Then we added some bigger ones so that it was filling the middle of the pit.

The four of us sat on the log, watching the flames. Dad took out a cigarette and lit it. Taking a long, deep drag, he sighed as he exhaled.

"Smoking is bad," Johanna reminded him.

Michael and I picked up small sticks with glowing ends and pretended to smoke with him.

"Smoking is bad," Johanna repeated. "I'm tellin'."

She didn't have to. Mom was right behind us.

"Why are you teaching them to smoke?"

"I'm not," he gasped. "It's not like they are smoking real cigarettes."

"It's bad for you," she continued.

"So we have been told," he retorted. He had been trying so hard to quit but had not succeeded yet.

"Well enjoy it," she said sarcastically. "Johanna, it's bed time." Mom took her by the hand and led her off into the dark, leaving us to be men in the firelight.

"When did you start smoking, Dad?"

"A long time ago."

"Really?"

"Yeah, started smoking straw first, but that's not really smoking..." This was more info than he should have given us.

"...then, I used to roll up leaves in a paper bag, but that's not really smoking either..." Way more info.

"...then cigarettes in the Army, that was smoking, tobacco in cigarettes...now I'm addicted and can't quit."

"What's bad about it?"

"Gives you cancer or all kinds of other lung diseases, people fall asleep smoking and set their beds or house on fire. Kills you one way or another..."

"...but once you are addicted, it's almost impossible to stop."

"Why did you start?"

"Government said it was all right, Army gave them to us for free in the war...damn government."

"Damn government," Michael and I repeated.

He stood up and stretched. "You let the fire die down and then put it out with that bucket of water, all right."

"How come water puts out a fire?" I asked.

"It smothers the oxygen."

"Huh?"

"It stops the oxygen from getting to the wood."

"What if there's bubbles in the water?"

"The bubbles burst and the water smothers the fire out."

"Like dropping a rock on a rat," Michael input.

Dad looked at him. "Huh?"

"When the rock hits the rat, he gets smothered and 'is legs stick out the sides, so he can't get away."

"Does that really work?" I asked.

"If you use a big enough rock," Michael said nodding.

Dad started to walk away, shaking his head. "Put it out in a while."

"All right," we both promised.

"I'm going in for a while but will check it later."

He left without another word.

This was great. A fort, a fire and our freedom. Freedom is a wonderful thing. Freedom to be your self. Freedom to think. Freedom to experience new things. Freedom to plan.

"Want to build another fort tomorrow?" Michael asked.

"Why? We have this one."

"This is yours. I want one too."

"Sure. Where?"

"In my dad's barn."

"You sure?"

"Yeah. I'm allowed."

"You sure?"

"Yeah. At the top, away from where they are taking the bales out."

"Tomorrow morning?"

"After chores?"

"I'll be there."

The fire had died down and so we took the bucket of water and poured it over the red coals. There was a hissing sound and steam mixed with the smoke. We both started coughing and our eyes started to water. Tiny thermal explosions from the colder water hitting the hot coals had thrown soggy ash all over our shoes.

We prodded the remains with a stick. No more glowing coals could be seen. The day was over. It was time to go to bed. We had big plans for the next day. As I walked to my bedroom, with my hands in my pockets, my fingers curled around the book of matches. That had been a great day.

I finished my chores around 10am the next day. Mom and Dad were busy doing something, somewhere, so I yelled bye to Granny.

"Granny, I'm going over to Michael's to help him build a fort."

"Don't get in trouble," she yelled back, from the kitchen window.

"Don't worry." I tried to sound reassuring as I broke into a run up the driveway.

"Famous last words," she said, but I didn't hear her. I had work to do and was already gone from earshot.

Michael was just coming up from the cow barn as I came into the farmyard. His blonde hair tussled from sleep.

"You ready?" he called out.

"Let's go."

The hay barn was open on all sides. Steel beams formed the framework of the barn and it had a steel roof. The bales of hay were stacked twenty-four high, sixty-four long and thirty-five deep. Farmer Day and his helper, Chris, took the hay from the end closest to the cow barn first. Most of the barn was full and only half of the first ten rows had been removed.

We walked around first, inspecting each side for the best area to build in. Michael had been thinking about this all night and had come up with a couple of really good ideas.

He needed to be able to get to one open side, without being seen. This would allow him to "smother" rats. Without being seen was important as the rat bait used were eggs stolen from the big hen house.

Next, he thought it would be a good idea if the fort had an emergency exit. This was sheer brilliance. One never knew what could happen. It was decided that the emergency exit would open up into the area where the hay was being removed. There were always loose piles of hay in there to land on safely.

This meant that the fort had to be built at the top of the stack, near the back wall, close to the area being worked. But we were not to be near the area being worked. That meant we had to build a tunnel for the emergency exit.

We also knew that at the top of the stack, under the curve of the roof, was an open section where no bales where stacked. We could build up there to our hearts' content. By removing certain bales from the outside row, we could create a way to climb up to the top. The bales we removed had to be put in the area being worked.

"Can't have hay bales laying all over the place." Michael sounded like his dad when he made that statement.

It took us about an hour but we managed to create the stairs, with giant steps up to the top. Farmer Day came by once and yelled at us, 'cause three of the bales we threw down split open. He made us pick up all the loose stuff and throw it in the working area. He wasn't that mad and even got us a couple of pitchforks to use. The three-pronged forks really helped and we left them right were he said in the area where we put the broken open bales.

It made quite a big pile of loose hay and using foresight, Michael and I piled it below where the emergency exit was going to be. Nice soft landing. Everything was going along fine.

Making our way up the giant stairs, we reached the area that seemed best to build. Pulling up bales of hay, we moved them around to make walls up to the steel roof. The back wall opened up and we could see all the way to the backfields, on the other side of the river, where it made the turn into the forest.

Turning the bales to make a back wall and we left an opening for "rat smothering". That was one requirement taken care of. We were ready to start on the tunnel, when we heard Michael's mom call.

"You two want some lunch?"

"Yes, please," Michael called back.

"Thought so, come down, I brought sandwiches."

Michael took off down the giant stairs and soon returned. His mom had been most thoughtful and placed some sandwiches and a couple of pops in a big tin box that used to hold "tea biscuits". He took the lid off and we wolfed them down, guzzled the pops, and then got right back to work.

The tunnel was easy to make. We just pulled up bales leading away from the one wall and laid them sideways over the hole we were creating, all the way to the open area. It came out almost directly above the pile of loose hay.

The last thing to do was hide the outside openings. Michael took out his penknife and cut one bale open. I had one too, but couldn't use it for a while due to an unfortunate accident with Norman's bike tire.

Because it was pressed together, by the baling machine in the field, we could pull off a part of the bale and push it into each of the openings. Then we climbed down and had a look. Nobody could tell where the emergency exit or the rat hole was.

We were done.

Michael ran to his house and came back with a couple more pops. Then we climbed up to sit in his new fort and relax.

"This is better than my glass fort," I said admiring our work.

"No it's not."

"Sure it is."

"No, yours has a fire pit."

We both took a big swig of pop.

"Your dad said that every fort needs a fire pit, remember."

"Yeah."

"So, it's not as good as yours."

This was the point that my above average intelligence kicked in.

"Hey," I spurted, "I know what to do."

Michael perked up right away.

"The biscuit tin," I pointed out, "won't burn. That could be the contained area. We could have a small fire in that."

"Really?"

"Yeah, we could save a little pop to put it out with."

"Yeah. Your dad said as long as the fire was contained it would be safe."

Michael grabbed a small handful of hay and I got out the matches from my pocket. He scrunched the hay into a small ball and put it in the tin. I lit the match and held it to the hay.

Presto, we had a small and very smoky fire. It didn't last very long and stayed inside the tin box. I threw the match in the tin box too.

"There ya go. Now you have a real fort."

He had a huge grin on his face. Wait until I told my dad how we had done this so safely. He would be so proud that I had remembered everything.

Then the fire went out. A small cloud of smoke hung in the enclosed area.

"Hey," Michael said, "you want to try smoking some straw. Your dad said it's not really smoking."

"Sure, but all we have is hay."

"Still grass. Hay and straw are really the same."

He had a good point there and after all, his dad was a farmer so he should know. We each got a piece of hay and I lit another match.

We lit our hay and leaned back against the walls of the fort to enjoy our smokes. Sucking on the hay, nothing happened except we burned our fingers, as each strand burst into flames. We both threw the flaming stalks into the tin box at the same time.

"Well, that sucked," he exclaimed.

"Probably works better with straw," I told him.

"Wanna have another fire?" he asked reaching for another handful of hay.

"Sure." I was already reaching for the matches.

We lit another small ball of hay. It burned very quickly and produced more smoke.

Michael coughed in the smoke. "Open the rat hole for air."

I pulled open the rat hole and smoke started to filter out. That was better.

Michael put some more scrunched up hay on the glowing remains. It started to glow red but no flames.

Again my brain was working. "Not getting enough oxygen at the bottom."

I leaned forward to blow on it. Took a deep breath and blew. The fire got oxygen immediately and burst into flames and more smoke.

"Cool." Michael was impressed that I knew what to do.

As the flames subsided he grabbed another handful of hay and threw it into the tin. This time, something unexpected happened.

As the hay flew loosely into the box, the flames ignited it in mid-air. The heat from the fire below created hot air that was rising from the biscuit tin, causing the flaming hay strands to rise into the air, landing on fire, outside the box.

All around us, hay bales where catching on fire and more little flaming strands of hay were rising, from these new fires to float away and start another.

I grabbed the lid of the tin box and started to beat at the small fires around me, in a futile attempt to put them out. Quick thinking Michael grabbed off his shoe and did the same. It was really starting to get smoky now. We also heard help coming up into the barn.

"Fire in the hay. Fire in the hay!" yelled Chris, as he made his way to us.

Michael yelled back, "We're trying to put it out."

Then we heard Farmer Day from down below. "You boys get out of there, now."

We didn't need to be told twice. We were sweating, either from fear of being burned up or from the spanking that had to follow this.

Michael yelled, "Emergency exit."

"Right behind you."

He disappeared down the smoky tunnel just as Chris pulled down the wall. He had a fire extinguisher in each hand and started spraying the small fires, putting them out.

I followed Michael down the tunnel. He had pushed out the sheath that we used to block the hole and had jumped. He looked smaller down there and I suddenly realized how high we really were.

"Jump!" he yelled.

I aimed for the pile of loose hay and launched myself into the air. Feeling the hay starting to envelop me I knew that it was not going to hurt. Then I felt my rear end hit something hard.

Everything started to move slowly.

The tines of a pitchfork suddenly shot up out of the

loose hay about four feet to my right. Then the shaft appeared. The sharp tines kept moving up and arcing over the top of me.

Farmer Day was looking up in the direction of the smoking hole.

Chris's voice sounded slurred as he cursed the fires and the two imbeciles who had caused it.

The tines were flying past my body now and moving through the air towards Farmer Day.

Michael yelled, "Look out!"

And then we watched as Farmer Day turned his head towards the flying pitchfork, just as the tines stuck into his leg, just above the knee.

A loud roar of pain and several curse words that I had not heard before exploded from him.

"Run!" yelled Michael.

"You better!" roared Chris, as he prepared to jump from the emergency exit after putting out the flames.

We did.

Michael's dad roared with pain as he slid the forks from his leg. That was the last sound that I heard as I ran for my bedroom to hide.

The sounds of people yelling had me shaking. With the covers pulled over my head, I waited. Crying. It wasn't my fault. The fire had been contained. I had done everything to make it safe. Still, punishment was coming. It had to.

Johanna's voice made me jump. "Smoking is bad."

Wiping the blanket off my head, I yelled at her, "Shut-up and go away." Then I buried my head again as she slammed the door.

The outside door creaked as it opened. Again, when it closed.

Silence.

Footsteps, crossing the room.

Somebody sat on the edge of the bed, causing my body to roll towards their weight.

Must be Dad, Mom would have yelled already.

Their weight shifted and they sighed. "Nigel?"

"Yeah?"

"Give me the matches."

Reaching into my pocket, I pulled out the remains of the pack. Then thrust my hand out from under the covers, opening the fingers to relinquish them.

His fingers touched my hand as they were taken and I pulled my hand back under.

"Nigel?"

"Yeah?"

"Were you smoking?"

"Not really."

"Not really?"

"You said smoking straw was not really smoking."

"Did you have a fire?"

"A safe one."

"A safe one?"

"It was in a contained area and only a small one. You said that was the right way."

"A contained area?"

"The tin biscuit box."

"How did the barn catch fire?"

"Michael did it."

"How?"

"He threw more hay on and it caught fire in the air and then started floating around. We tried to smother it, but that made it worse."

"Mr. Day has been taken to the hospital!"

"That was an accident, he told us to put the pitchforks there and he told us to jump."

"You and Michael cannot play together anymore and Mr. Day said that you can't go to on his property anymore."

"How will I get to school?"

"Walk quickly through the farmyard."

"You going to spank me?"

"I have to."

"Why?"

"To teach you a lesson."

"Which one?"

"Not to play with matches, as they can start a fire and a lot of people can get hurt, killed even."

"I already learned that. Do you still have to?"

"Yes, it's to make sure you remember. And after you are to stay in your room until you are told you can come out."

There was another sigh. He hated doing this as much as I hated getting it. "Come out of there."

The spanking was over soon enough, even though it seemed to take forever. With the covers over my head, my rear end stinging hot, I cried myself to sleep. It wasn't my fault. It wasn't fair. It wasn't my fault.

It was five days before I was allowed to play outside

again. School was no fun as the other kids teased Michael and I. We could talk there without getting in trouble at home. After blaming each other for a couple of days, we made up. But what good would that do? We still couldn't play together.

A new weekend came and I was bored. Dad had put the glass windows away so they didn't get broken. That was Johanna's fault as she had taken to throwing stones at Norman. She ran in there to get away when he threw them back. Mom gave her the lecture about, "People who live is glass houses..." You know the one.

Dad was busy grooming one of his show dogs. This was hard work and took about four hours to do right. Johnny was in a particular mood and had already bitten Dad's hand once.

The tension filled the air of the room as I walked in and sat on the stool to watch. Johnny growled and snapped at the hand again.

"Don't you dare!" Dad threatened him.

"Hey, Dad."

"Nigel, I'm busy right now."

"There's nothing to do."

"Find something, please."

"Can I build a new fort?"

"Where?"

"I was thinking about a tree fort."

"No fire pit."

"Tree house?"

"Where?"

"The big tree over by the blackberry bushes."

"No, that's on the farm."

"Actually, it's on our side of the barbed wire."

"Stay off the farm!"

"I will. Thanks."

"Take your sister with you."

"What?"

"If she doesn't go, you don't."

"She'll get in the way and get hurt!"

"Nigel!"

Reluctantly I agreed, "Alright."

Johanna was only too eager to come.

"You just watch though," I told her.

That was fine with her, so far. We walked out to the tree to develop a plan. It was a big tree and I would need to build a ladder up the side to get to the lower branches, about eight feet up. Another two feet up were two branches that came out over the blackberry bushes on our side of the barbed wire. A plan was forming.

As I turned to go, Johanna asked, "Where ya' goin'?"

"We need wood, a hammer and nails."

All this stuff I could get easily enough and wouldn't get in to trouble taking. The nails and hammer came from the barn. By the side of the barn was a pile of old junk and wood that I could use.

Fortunately, there was an old wooden toboggan in the pile that I could use to load everything. It took me two trips pulling it over the grass cause one load was too heavy to pull. After about forty-five minutes I was ready to build.

Trampling a narrow path through the thorny bushes, I created a path to the tree. Then nailing some short pieces of wood onto the trunk, I started to create a ladder to climb up. Johanna sat on the pile of wood watching. Farmer Day came by and glowered at me.

He still frowned at me as I said "sorry" to him. Then he limped away.

About ten minutes later Michael appeared on the other side of the fence.

"What are you doing?"

Johanna answered first. "You guys can't talk to each other."

"Well then, you tell him that I'm building a tree house."

"He's building a tree house."

Michael left. I kept nailing more steps. Then he came back. Without saying a word he started pulling the old rusty, tin sheets of roofing from the pile of junk on his side of the tree.

When Farmer Day had replaced the roof over the pigpens, he had placed the old sheets there, leaning them against the old tree. Between each sheet was a pile of dried out, old leaves that had fallen from the tree.

Looking at each other, we smiled, but didn't say a word while we worked. If we did, Johanna would tell. We weren't breaking any rules and playing beside each other silently was better than playing alone.

Johanna spoke to him first, "What ya doin', Michael?"

"Building a base camp out of these sheets."

"You guys can't play together!"

"We're not," I explained. "He's on his place and I'm on ours. We're not even talking, you are."

The work continued in silence.

A little while later, Dad came out to see what was going on. So did Farmer Day. They both stood facing the tree and each other with their arms folded.

Only Johanna spoke. "They're not playing together and they're not talking."

Nobody said anything. They just stood there watching us for about five minutes. I noticed a silent smile pass between them before Dad went back to grooming and Farmer Day hobbled off to his tractor.

My steps had been nailed in place and I was starting to haul up boards to make the floor. Michael was busy pulling out some big sheets of plastic, probably used to wrap the new roofing in, that were wedged between the rusty tin sheets.

Most of my floor had been built by the time he got the plastic wrap loose.

"I want something to do," Johanna asked.

"Ask Michael if you can have that plastic," I called down while I kept nailing.

"Michael, can I have that plastic?"

"Why?"

"Nigel, why do you want it?"

"I don't, you do."

"Why do I want it?"

"For walls."

"For walls, Michael."

"I guess, come and get it."

"You can bring it over."

"No I can't. Not allowed. Remember?"

"Oh, yeah."

She slowly started picking her way through the brambles towards the barbed wire.

"Ouch."

"Ow."

"Nigel, help me."

"I can't. Remember."

"Oh, yeah."

That's when the crying started. "I'm stuck. You get it."

"You gonna tell?"

"No."

Very carefully she picked her way back through the bushes and sat on the toboggan again. By the time she got there, I had made my way down and retrieved the plastic from Michael. We had both smiled at each other. We had her now. It was her fault if she told on us for playing together or talking.

Climbing back up, the floor was finished in a hurry. Michael had his walls standing up and was putting on the roof. Nailing the plastic to a branch overhead was a little tricky, as I had to stand on tiptoe. With that done all that was left was to drape the plastic over the sides of the floor and I had a triangle-shaped tree house. One more piece for the back wall, and another for the front. Done.

Johanna had climbed up the homemade ladder and was sticking her head inside.

"Can I come up now?"

"You're already up."

"Help me get in."

After taking her arms and pulling her in the rest of the way, she took stock.

"There is nowhere to sit."

She was right. "Hold on, I have an idea."

Climbing down, I pulled the old toboggan under the front of the tree house. It had wooden runners nailed on the bottom, so I could stand it on its back end. The rope on the front had each end passed through a hole and secured with a knot on the backside.

"Hey Michael, can..." I started, when she cut in.

"I'm tellin'."

"You can't. It's your fault cause you wouldn't get the plastic. I'll tell on you."

There was a slight pause before she said, "Oh, yeah."

"Can I borrow your knife for a minute?"

Standing up through a hole in the roof. He grinned. "Sky light." The closed penknife came hurtling over the bushes.

"Cool, thanks."

Pulling the rope through the back a bit gave enough rope to put the knot on the top of the sled. Using a sawing motion, it was easy to cut the knot off.

"Incoming!" I called as I tossed the knife back over the bushes and through his skylight. He came up rubbing the top of his head.

"Thanks." Then he went back down.

Now the rope should be long enough.

"Johanna, catch the rope when I throw it up."

Out poked her head between the plastic sheets. It took five tries but she finally caught it. Once I was back up, I took the rope and hauled up the toboggan, tugging it under the plastic. Now we had a seat. As an added bonus, but mostly because I was envious of Michael's skylight, I took the rope off and tied it to a branch, throwing it over the side made a fireman's escape. Mine was better.

Michael wanted me to see inside his base camp. So I climbed down. He had built a special sliding back door so I could get in without being seen by crawling under the bottom strand of barbed wire. We also realized that he could climb up to the tree house and stay hidden by the blackberry bushes and the tree branches that were hanging down. We couldn't have planned this any better.

He had done a good job. The floor was covered in the old leaves and he had even made two separate piles of dry, crackling leaves to lie on. The skylight allowed enough sun in to see in the murky gloom.

"Look what I have!" he said proudly.

"Hey, that's a cigar."

"No it's not. Just some of these dried leaves rolled in brown paper."

"Looks like a cigar."

"Wanna try it?"

"Yeah, but…"

"It's not really smoking. Right?"

"Yeah, but my dad took away the matches."

"Chris dropped his lighter and I found it in the barn. See," he said as he pulled out the prize.

"What about her?" I asked, jerking a thumb upwards.

"We'll be quick and put it out."

"Let's do it."

He already had the lighter lit and was touching the flame to the end of his eight-inch, make believe cigar. The end burned red and a small flame appeared. Sticking the unlit end in his mouth, he sucked. The flame disappeared and he suddenly started choking and coughing. Smoke was coming out his moth and nose, his eyes watered immediately and tears ran from the corners. He quickly thrust it at me.

"Your turn." He gagged.

Taking the smoking paper in hand, I held it to my mouth and sucked. My lungs burned as the hot smoke seared them. My stomach convulsed inward suddenly, violently squeezing the air from my body. Smoke was pouring from my face and I was gagging and coughing with watering, red eyes, when Johanna poked her head in the back door.

"Can I see too?"

I threw the cigar away and hastily gasped, "No."

We both made for the back door and she backed out of the way.

Michael came up with the next course of action as I was still trying to suppress a cough and half choking on it.

"Can I see inside yours?"

Nodding, I pointed up. He went first and then Johanna, which allowed me to get some air. I felt dizzy and wanted to vomit. After he had pulled her in, I climbed up.

That had been close.

"Cool." Michael was admiring the place, sitting on the toboggan, but looking a little pale.

Johanna decided to show off. "Even has a fireman's escape." She showed him by throwing the rope down.

The branches were shaking and bending down with the combined weight of the three of us. But it seemed safe enough, as long as we didn't bounce around.

"Johanna, sit down," I chided, while sitting down on my knees between Michael and the back wall. She sat on the end of the toboggan, by the front wall.

"Remember, you can't tell," I coached her.

"I won't."

"You better not."

Michael had a funny look on his face. "You smell something?"

Johanna wrinkled her nose as I answered, "Smells like your dad is burning something."

"Yeah, wonder what?"

"Garbage maybe?"

"No, did that yesterday."

Johanna sat up straight. "Smoke."

We both turned to her quickly and rebuked her sudden outburst, "No, we didn't!"

"Smoke!" she yelled pointing at the grayish colored cloud rising past the door opening by the tree trunk behind me.

Suddenly, the entire tree house was engulfed in thick, choking smoke. Leaning over to look down the tree, I could see smoke and flames coming out of every crack of the base camp. Then the wind blew a huge cloud into my face, obscuring the ground below and blinding me.

Panicked, I yelled the obvious, "FIRE!"

Michael jumped up to look and the house started to shake.

"Emergency exit!" he yelled.

My first thought was to save my little sister. My foot kicked out at the toboggan. It was all that it needed.

The last I saw of Johanna was her wide eyes full of shock and surprise as the plastic parted and the old sled shot out through the front wall, then she disappeared straight down, light blond hair flying up past her ears.

There was a thud. She screamed. Then she started crying loudly.

Michael and I slid down the rope, coughing and sputtering in the smoke.

We could hear our dads and Chris calling out through the smoke as we found her lying in the brambles, crying and yelling that she hated us.

"Over here!" I yelled.

Michael was trying to lift Johanna, but her leg was bent funny and it hurt her too much to move. My dad got there first.

"I found them," he yelled.

Picking Johanna up, he ushered the two of us in front of him. The thorns from the bushes scratched at the uncovered skin on our arms and faces, as he pushed us out from the middle of the brambles. Once clear of the smoke, he set Johanna down.

"Glyn?" my mother screamed as she ran towards us.

"It's all right, I have them," he called back.

Michael and I stood there in torn clothes, coughing, gagging, crying and bleeding. His mom and dad came running into the paddock. Dad was looking at Johanna's leg, as they all arrived.

"Her leg is broken," he told them.

Mom started to cry. Michael's mom put her arm around her.

"Don't fret," she told Mom, "they are all safe."

Mom glared at me. So did Dad. Michael's parents did the same to him.

"Not for long," I mumbled.

Dad scooped Johanna up and carried her to the car. Mom and Mrs. Day took her to the hospital. Chris had called the fire department as the blaze was out of control and the entire tree and fence line was now burning.

Our fathers had hold of each of us by an arm. We weren't getting away with this. We were made to watch as the fire trucks arrived, hoses rolled out and firemen started pouring water on the blaze.

It all made sense now. Oxygen was supplied by the wind and water smothered the fire. Huge clouds of steam mixed with the smoke as the huge fire was slowly extinguished. It was so interesting and exciting to watch, I forgot about the punishment that would follow.

A fireman in a white hat came over and reported that the fire had started at the base of the tree, in amongst some old tin roofing.

"Somebody must have thrown a match or cigarette in there as they walked by," he commented while looking at Chris, who just happened to be lighting a cigarette with a match.

He shook his head quickly, "Not me, haven't been around there all day."

Our dads looked at us. We both hung our heads.

Turning silently on their heels, our fathers marched us home. Dad was moving so fast, his hand clenched tightly around my arm, that my feet barely touched the ground all the way to my room. The door slammed shut behind us.

I tried to explain, but this time he would not listen. His face was beet red as he looked at me.

Off came his belt.

I turned around and bent over. I had the feeling that this time it was going to hurt me more than him.

Mom returned with Johanna about two hours later. I could see her out the bedroom window of my new "prison cell" as she was carried to her room, sucking on an ice cream.

As she saw me, she yelled, "SMOKING IS BAD!"

With a whispering voice that nobody could hear but me, I answered, "I know that now. So is spanking."

Cruft's Ice Cream Party

"Now calling to Ring # 3, Number 415, Number 719, Number..."

We were at Cruft's Dog Show in London. One of the most important dog shows in the world. This was the biggest event of the year for my dad. He bred Standard Schnauzers and for the past ten years, his male, Champion Sundays Boy of Allbright, (we called him Soda), had been the best and was one of the last remaining champions.

Nobody else's dogs could beat him. In order for a dog to become a champion, it had to beat other champions. Soda had won so many shows that nobody else was making champion. The other breeders were very angry and went to the British Kennel Club to ask them to force Dad to retire Soda.

They couldn't force Soda's retirement, but they did make my dad mad. He made a deal with them all.

"The first time another male Standard beats Soda to make champion, I will retire him, on the spot!"

They all agreed.

What they didn't know was that Dad already had a new dog that he had found in Germany. His name was Artus Von Klusenstein; his real name was too long to say, so we called him Johnny. At the time the deal was made, Johnny was in the quarantine area of Customs waiting to come to Carpenter's.

Nobody had seen him except Dad. Johnny had belonged to the German police force and was very well trained in everything.

His first show was to be at Cruft's, the biggest show of the year. Every breeder was going to be there.

So was Soda.

Norman was old enough to stay home at a friend's house; Mom and Dad brought Johanna and me to the show.

Johnny and Soda were in separate stalls, beside each other, because males had a habit of fighting, and Johnny had an attitude problem. Soda was sound asleep and I was curled up against him, with my head on his ribs, sleeping also. It had been a long day already.

Dad listened to the ring call, "That's Johnny's number being called."

"Ooo…," said Mom holding Johanna in her arms, "I want to see this!"

"Leave Nigel to sleep," Dad said confidently. "Soda will look after him."

That was the thing about Standard Schnauzer's, they were originally bred as herd dogs, and were very loyal. They knew their family and protected it.

They left without another thought, secure in the knowledge that I was safe.

It must have been a wonderful dream, even if I didn't remember it, I was in a deep, deep sleep.

Somebody was too close to the stall.

Suddenly, Soda jumped to his feet, protectively, standing over me. My head jerked upwards as he stood up and then abruptly fell downwards.

Thud.

It hit the floor of the wooden stall. Wide-awake and very disorientated, I tried to sit up quickly, only to smack my head into Soda's stomach.

I heard him growling.

He jumped to get out of the way of my heads intrusion. I kept trying to sit up.

I heard someone say, "Whoa…!"

With the same sitting up motion, I was moving forward to get out of the stall, my head and shoulders leaning forward, to lead the way. That's when Soda decided that he better do his job, as the rest of the family was missing.

There was a blur in front of my eyes.

Warm breath on my face.

Something hairy tickled my cheek.

My nose suddenly felt wet.

Then it was pinched by something sharp.

A woman screamed.

Soda dragged me back into the stall with his mouth clamped onto my nose. I had no choice but to turn my head and fall backwards, twisting over and rolling behind him.

"Owww!" I yelled as I reached for my nose, tears starting from the shock.

Soda was growling at the two people trying to come to my aid.

I thumped him in the ribs. "Stupid dog!"

He twitched but didn't move from his protective stance against the outsiders.

Dad came running up at that exact moment, "What's

wrong?"

"That dog," the lady gasped, "bit that little boy's face."

Soda saw my dad and started wagging his back end, which in turn was hitting me in the head.

"Nigel?" Dad called.

"Yeah?"

"You all right?" he asked as he pushed Soda out of the way.

"Yeah?" The tears had stopped but my nose still hurt.

"What happened?"

The couple stood close enough to hear, but stayed back from Soda, who had turned to licking my face with a big wet tongue, the beard on his chin tickled my cheek, again. Explaining how I had woken up and hit my head, then trying to get out of the stall, of Soda biting my face, but not about thumping him, he chuckled.

"He was just trying to protect you," he explained as he looked at my nose.

Mom came back with Johnny and Johanna, as he was explaining to the couple that everything was all right. Soda hadn't really hurt me. The skin wasn't even broken. He was just doing what came naturally. They left and Mom started laughing about the whole thing.

"Yeah, very funny," I said under my breath.

Soda was nuzzling and licking the back of my neck, as she put a cheap Band-Aid over the teeth marks on my nose and gave me my glasses. Dad took me for an ice cream.

Everything went along smoothly for a while. Dad was able to show the dogs in their respective rings. There were a lot of dogs there. Johnny and Soda were not competing head to head yet. But they were both winning which meant that they might later. They both had to win each ring they were in to be in the finals. Then, if Johnny beat Soda and the rest of the winners, he would be able to make champion, in one show.

I was getting bored. Walk to the ring. Johnny wins. Walk back to the stall.

Walk to the ring. Soda wins. Walk back to the stall.

Walk to the ring...

At least Johanna got carried back and forth by Mom. The last time for each one was coming up.

"Dad, I'll stay here with Soda this time."

"Sure?"

"Yeah."

That was all it took to get Johanna started.

"I wanna stay too," she demanded, jumping up and down beside me.

"You," I said, as I gave her a shove sideways, "are too small."

It wasn't done on purpose. She just happened to be in mid jump, when I pushed her. I still think she tried to dramatize the fall, but the end result was that as she fell, she hit her face on the side of the stall.

A trickle of blood ran down her cheek from the side of her right eyebrow.

"Nigel!" Mom gasped, picking up her crying, bleeding darling. She told me off and said she would be right back after she cleaned Johanna up in the bathroom.

Dad looked down at me. "Be more careful, please."

"Sorry. Can I stay here?"

"Yeah, I guess, just be good."

"I will. I promise."

He took off with Johnny to the ring, leaving me alone with Soda.

Sitting on the edge of Soda's stall, swinging my legs under me, I was reveling in the attentive comments of passersby.

"What a good dog." "What a cute boy." "Isn't that sweet."

Yes I was. Thank you very much. Move along, fatty. Nice hairdo!

The sound of the ring caller's voice was just another noise in the murmur of the crowd and hundreds of barking dogs.

"Hey," said the Pug breeder across the aisle, "wasn't that your dog's number?"

"What?"

Soda's arm band and number was hanging on the edge of the stall where Dad had left it. Number 339 stamped on it in big black numbers.

"That was the second call for number 339."

"Dad will be back for the final call."

"All right."

He should have been back by now. Where are Mom and the brat? Soda could sense my apprehension and stood up beside me. Scanning the aisle for my parents, I heard what I didn't want.

"Final call for number 339 to Ring 6. Final call for number 339 to ring 6."

The Pug man looked at me.

I looked down the aisle. No sign of them. Looking at the Pug man, I shrugged my shoulders.

"What can I do?"

"Get him to the ring quickly!" he said.

"What? ME?"

"Yeah, quick put on the arm band and get in the ring, before he is disqualified."

He started waving his arms at me to move faster, the grooming comb in his hand acting like a flag. Other breeders around us were starting to realize what was happening. The woman with the Great Danes came over and started to do up my shirt buttons.

"Must look presentable."

Then she grabbed the number band and tried to put it on my arm. It was too big or my skinny arm was too small, the number wrapped all the way around and all you could see was 39.

"This won't work!" she exclaimed looking around for help.

The flamboyant guy with the fuzzy Afro hair that my dad referred to as "Mary" plucked a very large, pink hair clip from the Poodle he was working on.

Rushing over, he said, "Here," and grabbing the number, used the hair clip to pin it to my shirt pocket, "that will have to do."

The older couple with the Beagles looked concerned. Then the gentleman jumped up. "I'll tell them your on your way, they'll wait a couple of more minutes." He disappeared into the crowd.

The Great Dane lady reached for Soda's leash and he

barked at her, making me jump. "You get him."

"I've never done…"

"Get him, NOW!" she ordered.

I grabbed Soda's leash and he jumped out of the stall. The Pug guy came over, loosening his tie, he pulled it off, over his head.

"You have to wear a tie in the ring," he said as he slipped it over my head, under my collar and tightened it around my neck. It was too long and hung down past the crotch of my pants.

"Tuck the end in your pants."

With the tie tucked in I started off down the aisle with Soda at my side, heeling perfectly.

"This way!" someone yelled.

Turning quickly the other way, I snapped, "Soda Heel."

He did a perfect turn. All those days my dad made me walk the dogs and learn the proper commands were going to be needed now.

I heard someone whisper; "Did you see that!"

The Great Dane lady was leading the way to the ring for me. The crowd parting in front of her as she called loudly, "Dog coming through. Dog coming through."

The crowd parted and stared at the strange sight of the seven-year-old boy. Wearing thick glasses and a Band-Aid on his nose, a tie that was far too big and a very large pink clip to hold a show number on his shirt that seemed to cover the majority of his chest. While leading a large, salt and pepper colored dog, with a four-inch beard and eyebrows, that was almost as big as the child and walked with a definite attitude.

We reached the ring and the two Stewards stared at my number and waved me in.

There were eight other Standard Schnauzer's waiting in a line on the far side of the ring. The judge was standing at the far end of the line waiting impatiently.

They all looked at me.

I looked at the Great Dane lady and shrugged.

She waved me in and the man handling the dog at the closest end of the line, pointed beside him. Soda walked at a perfect heel beside me as I walked to my place in the line. This was his element and had done this so many times he knew what to do.

I started sweating.

No problem, I thought. *What would Dad do? Come on Nigel, you've watched him do this. What would he do?*

Reaching the end of the line, I turned Soda to stand in the same direction as the others. Then stood facing his right side.

A voice from behind me said, "Hold the leash on a short chain above his head, Nigel."

As I turned to see my godfather, Donald Becker, pushing through the crowd behind, he said, "Don't look at me. Look at Soda."

Quickly I turned about. Uncle Donald was here. Everything would be all right.

Sweat was beading up all over my face. My glasses started to slide down my nose.

Soda held his head up and I held the shortened leash over his head.

"Use your fingers to comb his beard down," Uncle

Donald directed.

Switching hands holding the leash, I ran the fingers on my right hand through the soft beard, so that it hung down nicely.

"Square up his back legs."

The leash switched hands again.

His left leg was further back than his right. So I reached down with my left hand and pushed his left foot forward.

"No," said Uncle, "Leave that one. Move the right one back!"

The judge had looked at all the other dogs and reached Soda just as I stood up. As he started to look at Soda, Uncle said, "Hold his head up and lift his tail up."

"What?" I whispered out of the corner of my mouth.

The breeder standing beside me whispered, "Hold his head and tail up."

Soda's head was up but my arm was too short to hold his tail. I just couldn't reach it. So I stood on one leg and tipped his tail upward with my left foot. That was when one side of the Band-Aid let go, my glasses slide further down, pushing the strip ahead of them, which looked like I had a small plastic tongue protruding from the end of my nose.

The judge was a distinguished looking man, a little portly with a soft voice.

"What happened to your nose?" he asked quietly, while running his hand along Soda's back.

"My dog bit me, sir."

"Which dog?"

"This one, sir."

He removed his hand quickly. My legs were starting to shake a little, which made me wobble, but didn't fall.

"Why?"

"He was protecting me, sir."

"And he bit you?"

"Accident, sir. He is really a very good, loyal and obedient dog. Just doing his job, sir."

He nodded approval and turned away. Signaling to the first breeder to start running around the ring with his dog. Then the next followed by the next and so on.

"Nigel," came Uncle's voice, "stop standing on one leg and get ready to run him around. Remember to hold his head up."

This I could do. I'd seen Dad do it before. It was easy, just run in a big circle beside Soda. The dog beside us started running. I let them get a head start.

"Soda, Heel."

Then I started running. Soda trotted beside me. Pushing my glasses back up my nose with the Band-Aid flapping about, we ran around the end, down the other side of the ring, across the bottom end. Almost back to where we started. Almost done. I could see Uncle Donald smiling in the crowd.

Each dog stopped in the position they started from. We rounded the last corner, ten more feet, I waved to Uncle as we ran past and smiled.

Soda stopped on cue, as I tripped over my own feet. My knees hit first and then my hands landed in front of me. Glasses skidded off my face, under the dog in front and out into the ring.

The judge was walking back down the row, taking one last look at the dogs before announcing the winner. Soda was standing perfectly as I stood up behind him. The portly judge leaned forward as I appeared from behind my dog and handed me my glasses.

"Thank you, sir," I said, quickly taking them in one hand and trying to hold Soda's head up with the other.

He nodded and walked away to the Steward's table. After writing in a book for a moment. He returned to the center of the ring with three ribbons, to announce First, Second and third Place.

"Third Place, Number 553."

The breeder ran the dog forward to collect the ribbon.

"Second Place, Number 224."

They collected theirs.

"First Place," he looked at Soda and I as he walked over, "Number 339."

The crowd roared in approval as he handed the ribbon to me and whispered.

"Nice job young man, Best Standard I've seen today."

"Thank you, sir."

Proudly I walked Soda out of the ring. Mom was waiting with Johanna as we exited. She had the biggest smile on her face.

"Nobody was there to do it!" I said, handing Soda's leash to her.

"You did fine. Go tell Dad."

Pushing through the crowd in the aisle I made my way towards our stalls looking for him. He was standing in front of the stalls, Johnny on a leash beside him. Uncle

Donald was shaking his hand, smiling and the two were laughing. I heard the last part of what Uncle was saying as I ran up.

"…could beat everyone standing on one leg, he could!"

"We won, we won!" I yelled as I jumped up on his back in enthusiasm, grabbing onto his shoulders.

What happened next is a bit of a blur. I felt something sharp dig into my right shoulder, something heavy hit me in the back.

I was moving backwards rapidly, the concrete floor was coming at my face and a growling, and snarling sound was in the air.

Dad shouted, "Johnny, NO."

I hit the ground hard and the heavy weight was removed from my back, as my glasses sailed under the stalls. Dazed but unhurt I rolled over to Dad pulling Johnny back.

"Johnny, no!" he said again. "Nigel, are you all right?"

"Yeah, I think."

Checking myself over as Uncle helped me stand up, I discovered that the back of my shirt had been ripped away at the shoulder.

"Why did he do that?" I asked indignantly.

"He thought you were attacking me and was just doing his job."

"How come they have to keep doing their job?"

"It's bred into them, Nigel, just like breathing is in you."

"Can we pull out their teeth then?"

"No," he laughed, "he'll get to know you better and then he'll protect you too."

"Like Soda?"

"Like Soda."

"Oh no! That's all I need."

"You won with Soda."

"Yeah."

"Now they are both in the finals, Nigel."

"Do I have to do that again?"

"Do you want to?"

"No thanks, too much running around."

Mom had returned by then and everyone started laughing. Johnny was forgiven and I was a hero. Both dogs were in the finals. Life was good.

Uncle Donald took Soda into the final and Dad took Johnny. All the other owners showed up to watch. It was quite a display and Johnny won, with Soda second.

Johnny made Champion in one show.

Dad walked out of the ring and with Johnny by his side went to the table of officials from the Kennel Club. They looked up as he approached.

"Johnny, sit," he commanded.

Then he addressed the British Kennel Club, "I would like to announce the retirement of Champion Sundays Boy of Allbright, otherwise known as Soda."

The man looked very smug as he wrote down the retirement notice.

"And," Dad continued pointing down at Johnny, "I would like to introduce you to Champion Artus Von Klusenstein."

The man glared at him furiously.

"Beat this one!" Dad finished.

We watched him walk back to us, a smile pasted all

over his face and a laugh in his step. Johnny trotted beside with the attitude of a true champion.

"Hey Dad," I blurted out, "ice cream?"

"For everyone."

Even Johnny and Soda had ice cream in a bowl. One on either side of the bench we sat on.

Dad said we could even eat cake.

Evil KerPluckrose

"Nigel, are you sure about this?"

Matthew's father had taken us to see the Motorcross racing that Saturday. It was fantastic. Motor bikes of all different sizes racing around the course at the old military training grounds.

They raced around corners, up and down hills, through shallow rivers, mud flying, launching into the air over jumps. Crashing into bushes, hay bales, the ground and each other. It was loud, dirty, gasoline smelling, fast, little boy and grown men fun.

One rider was dressed all in black and had his name across the shoulders of his leather suit. The sign on his trailer said he was a stunt rider and at 3pm would jump his motor bike up a ramp, over thirteen cars and land on a second ramp. We watched him fly through the air and when he landed the crowd went wild cheering.

He rode his bike back past the roaring crowd with the front wheel up in the air. He kept that "wheelie" up for the entire ride past.

That was when I decided that I was going to be a stunt rider.

Matthew's dad told us all about being a stuntman on the way home. I was amazed to learn that a stuntman could do just about anything; crashing a car into a wall, riding a motorbike, fighting, jumping off buildings, walking on the wing of an airplane, setting themselves on fire, just about anything you could think of!

It sounded perfect to me, except the part about setting myself on fire. That was not so appealing. The more I thought about it on the way home, the more excited I got. This had to be what my dad referred to as, "a defining moment in life."

We were waiting for my parents to come and pick me up at Matthew's and so I broached the subject with him.

"What do you think?" I asked Matthew.

"Not my cup o' tea, but if that's what you want."

"Yeah, it is."

So it was that I convinced him to help me start to practice. First we had to build a ramp in just the right place.

The right place was easy to pick. It was the bottom of his driveway. Since there was a steep slope from the sidewalk down to his garage door, I thought that this would enable me to gain enough speed for the jump. The garage door would act as my crash bumper to stop me.

The ramp was also easy to build as we found his neighbour had enough boards. We just grabbed four and leaned them against some bricks that we found in the other neighbor's back yard. We had the ramp built in no time.

Matthew had a new bike and I was planning to use this to ride.

"Are you nuts?" he asked. "My new bike? No, find something else!"

"What you got then?"

Disappearing through the side door of the garage, he reappeared pushing an old pram. It had four good rubber wheels mounted on steel rims. The handle at the back would allow him to give me a good push off, while running and the hood folded down at the back. The body of the pram was big enough that if I could sit in it with my knees bent.

Perfect.

Everything was lined up perfectly and we sent the pram down empty, for a test run. It rolled down the slope, up over the boards and gave a hop over the jump, finally coming to a halt by banging into the garage door with, a louder than anticipated, bang.

"Oy!" his father yelled. "What are you doing?"

"Nothing," Matthew called back.

"Well knock off that noise!"

"Okay."

"Now what?" Matthew asked.

"Not a problem," I answered. "Just point the pram towards the bush."

"Huh?"

"I can crash into the bush, just like the guys in the race. No noise."

I must have made sense because he agreed. We got the pram back up to the top of the drive and I climbed in. After watching the empty pram on its test run, I decided that I would need more speed to make a proper jump.

Matthew pulled the pram out on to the street so that he could get a good run before the top of the driveway slope.

"Ready?" he asked.

"Evil KerPluckrose will now attempt an almost impossible jump." I started the commentary, which is very important to every stunt. "This will be a death-defying jump over…Hey, I'm not jumping over anything."

Matthew was starting to get the idea. "Hold on," he said as he ran in the house. When he came back, he was carrying three beautiful dolls. Laying the dolls down behind the jump for the pram to go over, he shouted, "There."

"I'm ready," I yelled. "Let's go."

Back up the hill he came and started pushing the pram for the slope. I held onto the sides as it rocked on the old springs.

"Aim for the bush when you let go," I reminded him.

"GO!" he shouted as he let go.

Down the slope I raced.

The ramp racing toward me.

It didn't look lined up right.

Too much to one side.

The wheels on the left side missed the ramp, but the wheels on the right didn't.

The pram was launched up on two wheels, as I held onto the sides with the bush ahead. The right side wheels jumped over all the dolls, but now I was turning too much to the left. I was going to miss the bush and hit the…

SMASH.

Glass went flying everywhere as the pram and I sailed through the plate glass window beside the front door of Matthew's house, just as my horrified parents pulled to a stop at the curb.

The pram finally bounced onto its side and I spilled out onto the floor amongst the broken glass, landing at the feet of the astonished Matthew's father.

"What in blazes…?" he muttered.

"That didn't work right!" was all I could manage.

His face was starting to turn red as I started brushing the invasive glass from my clothes. Rolling over to get up, I could see my parents running down the driveway, through the remnants of what had been a nice, frosted window. Matthew still stood at the top with a stupefied look on his face.

"Nigel!" Mom called. "Are you all right?"

"Yeah."

"You cut?"

"Don't think so," I said looking for blood, without finding any.

"What happened?" asked my dad.

"Missed the bush."

Matthew had come down and using the door entered the front hall. "I told him not to!"

"No you didn't!" I exclaimed. "You helped push and you got the dolls."

"Dolls?" Matthew's mother blurted.

"Yeah, he got three dolls for me to jump over."

"My dolls!" she screamed as she ran outside.

"Where did you get the wood and the bricks?" asked his dad as his gaze followed his wife outside.

"Next door," I answered, "and the other next door."

He got a suspicious look on his face, as our ramp seemed vaguely familiar. "Show us?"

Matthew's mom came back in carefully holding her three, porcelain, antique dolls.

"I made it!"

Mom looked at me sternly, "Good thing!"

"Show us where you got that stuff," continued his dad.

Matthew led the way to the neighbor on the right. Our fathers stared at the gaping hole in the backyard fence, where we had pulled the boards off.

"They'll go back on," Matthew offered.

"That's not the point!" Bellowed his father. "The bricks?"

We led the way over to the other house and into the backyard. Nobody said anything. Then we pointed at the place from where we had borrowed the bricks. The hole in the brick patio wasn't that big and the bricks would go back, but again, that was not the point. Both our dads started telling us everything we had done wrong. How our lives, as we knew them were over and we were grounded for life. That we belonged on "Chain Gangs" for stealing.

"We didn't steal," I interjected, "we borrowed. We were going to put them back."

Dad grabbed me by an arm and spun me around. "Any time you take something, that belongs to someone else, without asking, it's stealing."

"Even if we were going to put it back?"

"Yes!" he yelled.

Matthew and I both answered at the same time, "Sorry."

They marched us back to Matthews's house, where our mothers were cleaning up the glass. Getting a hammer from the garage, they made us carry everything back to where it belonged. They nailed the boards back and replaced the bricks. Then they made us knock on each neighbor's door to confess our guilt.

The brick people were not home.

"Good thing," whispered Matthew, "he's not very nice."

The board man answered his doorbell. We explained what we had done, about the ramp and the smashed window and apologized. He tried to look very angry, but his eyes were smiling.

"Well, I hope you have learned your lesson," he said, staring down at us.

"Yes sir," we both mumbled.

As he closed the door, we could hear him laughing, "Marge, you're not gonna believe what just happened!"

It was not funny to us anymore.

My parents had placed me in the car and we were driving home. Everything was silent for a while.

Mom sounded exasperated as she asked, "Why?"

"I was practicing."

"To be a thief, a brick layer, a carpenter or a demolition man?"

"A stuntman," I answered proudly.

"Good Lord have Mercy…" Mom prayed.

"Well, at least we took the matches away." Dad chuckled, while trying hard to keep a straight face.

Mom stifled a snicker long enough to tell me that I was grounded to our property until further notice and that I would have extra chores until the window was paid off.

Arriving at Carpenter's, I was sent to my room to think about what I had done. Dad came in after about an hour and sat on the bed.

"Well?" he asked

"I'm sorry."

"About what?"

"Taking the bricks and boards without asking."

"How about the pram and the dolls?"

"Matthew got those, but I guess he should have asked too."

"And?"

"And for missing the bush."

"And?"

"Breaking the window?"

"And?"

"There's more?"

"How about scaring your mother half to death?"

"Really?"

"Yes."

"I'm sorry, I guess I didn't think about that."

"That's part of the problem, Nigel, you don't think things through."

"You gonna spank me now?"

"No, it doesn't seem to help."

"Can I go out and play now?"

"No. What ever gave you the idea to be a stuntman?"

I explained about the races and the guy who made the jump. How Matthew's dad had told us all about stuntmen and what they do for a living. About what I wanted to be when I grew up and that I was practicing.

He explained that being a stuntman is a very dangerous job and that I could get hurt. How every stunt is thought out precisely before being attempted. That a helmet must be worn and that each one of the stuntmen also wears pads to protect them. They tried to think of everything, so they don't get hurt. Did I not see that there was an ambulance and a fire truck there? Just in case something went wrong.

Did I understand how dangerous what I had done was?

"The pram didn't even have any steering!" he noted.

"You're right. I'm sorry."

"Do you understand? Really?"

"Yes. Can I go talk to Mom."

He nodded and sighed running his hands through his hair, not sure that I really did understand, but hoping. I went and found Mom. After telling her that I was sorry, that I didn't mean to scare her and that next time I would think about what I was doing, she hugged me.

"Be careful, please."

"I will."

Grounded to my room turned out to be a blessing. I was able to plan out my next stunt and gather all the protective equipment that I could.

Tomorrow, I would start with learning how to do a wheelie.

The next morning, during breakfast, I asked, "Can I go ride my bike?"

Dad looked up. "After you cut the grass."

"All of it?" After all we had ten acres.

"No, just the back, around the fruit trees, down past the rock garden and where the cherry tree is."

"That will take all morning!"

"Then you can ride your bike." He glared at me.

No use arguing. I knew that look.

After breakfast I went out to the barn and found the mini-tractor that we used to cut the grass. Dad had taught me how to operate it last year and I was a pretty good driver. It was a rusty, green color and a mower with two blades was mounted underneath it. It could pull a small trailer and we used it to do other small jobs too. A lever under the steering wheel, that required one to drive with a leg on each side, operated the three gears, one fast, one slow and reverse.

Starting in the back where Dad said, I started weaving in and out of the trees cutting the grass. This was boring work, but at least I got to practice my driving. Dad had promised he would teach me how to drive the minivan, once he knew that I could drive the tractor safely. Finished in the trees I worked at cutting around the rock garden, this was a little tricky due to the empty goldfish pond that surrounded it.

All that was left now was the big open space bordered by the fruit trees on each side. This was always the most boring part as I drove up towards the house, then down towards the rock garden. Turn around and do it again, and again and again. I couldn't even use the fast speed or the mower wouldn't cut properly.

It gave me lots of time to think.

If I took my bike up into the loft of our barn;

Then opened the upper doors that were used to bring up the hay;

And put up a board from the door to the top of the wooden fence;

Nailed another flat board onto the fence;

Angled the next board, just a little to miss the fence post, down to the ground;

Where a ramp was built;

I should be able to get enough speed to jump over something bigger than dolls!

Yeah, that should work! What have I missed? Protective padding, nope, had that. Permission, nope, I could do anything I wanted as long as I didn't do any damage to anything. Anything going to get damaged? Nope. Helmet? That was it! I needed a helmet. Well, my riding hat should work. It protects my head when I fall of the horse at riding lessons. Right? Right, that was settled.

Over and over and over, I drove back and forth cutting the grass. It took about an hour for this part. But it gave me time to go over my plans again and really think things through.

Finally finished, I raised the mower and got ready to drive around the house to do the part where the cherry tree was. Too bad Dad had been digging a ditch for a new sewer line. He was putting in a new bathroom with hot and cold running water. No more waiting for the kettle to boil for hot water and real flushing toilets.

Looking at the mound of earth along this side of the ditch, I wished he had waited. I used to be able to just drive over past the tanks that held our water supply. Pushing in the clutch, I changed gears to fast and started up towards the far side of the house.

I wonder.

I'm going pretty fast.

Maybe?

Impulse took over and I started heading towards the mound. I was going fast enough. I can make it. I know I can.

The front wheels of the little tractor ran up the ramp of dirt and into the air. I could look over the side and down into the ditch at the new pipe.

I was going to make it.

The front end went down and the wheels hit the ground, the bump knocking my foot of the gas pedal. They were over, but the lack of gas slowed the engine enough that the tractor slowed down, just a bit.

It was enough that the back wheels didn't quite make it over. They hit the far side of the ditch hard but were still turning. The sudden jolt bounced me up off the seat and I let go of the steering, the front wheels turned in a direction of their own choosing as the tractor continued forward.

It was like riding a bucking bronco. "Whoa!"

I was over. I made the jump. Reaching for the steering wheel I looked up just in time to see the front of the tractor smash into the trunk of the big, old cherry tree.

It stopped dead still, but I didn't.

Flying forward off the seat, the steering wheel hit me in the stomach, as the crotch of my pants sailed in to the gear levers.

Cherry blossoms dropped like snowflakes all over me, from the shaking but solid tree, as I groaned in pain.

The engine stalled.

Climbing slowly back into the seat, I realized that nobody had seen. That was lucky. Except for the big gash of missing bark on the tree, everything was all right. This was a good time for a drink of water. I started the tractor and drove over by the tanks.

Maybe just sit for a minute.

After a few minutes I was feeling much better. Got a quick drink of water from the tap and went back to cutting the grass. Dad was right. You have to think these things through all the way. About everything that could go wrong, padding and a helmet were definitely a necessity.

Mom came walking by, on her way down to the kennels, just as I was finishing.

"What happened to the tree?"

"Oh sorry, had an accident." No need to bother with details, if she didn't ask.

"Be more careful."

"I will. Can I ride my bike now?"

"Yes." And she went on her way.

The old barn was over on the other side of our property and I got my bike on the way, balancing on the side of the mower with one hand, driving slowly. It was on the other side of the chicken coops, behind the trees, on the other side of the trail that led down to the gate into the forest.

Parking the tractor in front, I dragged my bike up the stairs into the loft. As the doors opened I looked down. Should be high enough and a board from here to there, another along that portion of the fence top, down there to a ramp. Yep, that should do it.

Leaving the bike in the loft, I came down and had another look at it from the ground. Yeah, that is going to do the trick. Now, to work.

In no time I had found some boards out back of the barn that were the right length. Nailed one on top of the fence. Another leaned up to the loft doors and was nailed into place, the last angled around the fence posts a bit and down to the ground. About two feet of flat ground and another board going up, supported by some old buckets and a sawhorse made the ramp.

Almost ready! I beamed at my handiwork and thought how Dad would be proud of my foresight.

"Lunch time," called Granny from the kitchen window.

Johanna was almost finished by the time I got there. Norman had gone to fly radio controlled planes. Mom and Dad would eat when they had time.

"Take Johanna with you this afternoon, will you Nigel?" Granny suggested.

"Why?"

"Got some company coming soon and she'll get under our feet."

"But..."

"Please Nigel?" she asked.

"Yeah, take me with you."

"I'll make trifle for dessert," Granny bribed.

"All right, but I'm just going to the barn."

As we finished up our lunch the Gypsy wagon pulled up outside the house. They came every few months and an old lady in a shawl came in to visit with Granny. The men and a young girl always stayed with the wagon and Granny never said anything about her visit. It was all rather mysterious, but she was from Wales, everything there was mysterious. Granny used to tell us stories about the fairies that lived there.

First stop was my room. I put on four thick sweaters and shoved a piece of wood under them to protect my chest.

I put on my shin pads from cricket that protected my shins and knees. My riding cap for a helmet, and last thing, rolled up three pairs of socks, which I stuck down the front of my pants. I hadn't thought of these last night but after the accident this morning, they would help. That ought to do. It was all I had.

"What are you doing?" Johanna asked when I came back outside.

"Riding my bike," I answered as I started out for the barn.

"Why are you dressed like that?"

"Dad said."

"What?"

"That I should dress like this."

"Why?"

"Protection."

"From what?"

I stopped and turning around, snapped, "Will you shut up? I told you I am just going to the barn to ride my bike. Now it's important that you don't disturb me. I have to prepare."

"From what?"

"Dangerous stuff."

"I'm tellin'."

"On what? I haven't done anything."

"What's down your pants?" she asked pointing at the bulging zipper.

"Socks."

"Why?"

"I told you, protection."

"Why?"

"Look. I'm allowed to ride my bike. Dad told me to think things through and I did. He also told me about the importance of protection and I've got that. Are you coming or not?"

"Yes."

"Then let's go." I turned for the barn. It was about time. Granny better make trifle for dessert after this.

"What's this?" she questioned when she saw the ramps that I had built.

"Ramps."

"Why?"

"For jumping over things."

"Over what things?" she asked.

She had a point. I hadn't thought about what I would jump over.

"I have to think of something."

Johanna started to jump up and down excitedly, "Jump over me, jump over me."

I hadn't thought of that. It might be pretty good. Jumping over people. Sounded dangerous. Dangerous was stuntman work.

"All right. Come over here and lie down."

Leading her over to the jumping ramp I got her to lie down in front of it. Then standing back I had a look. Maybe she should be a little closer to the ramp. Mom would be really mad if she got hurt. Dad had said to think things through.

"No, over here, closer to the ramp. Yeah, now don't move."

"Where are you going?"

"Up to the hay loft."

"Why?"

"That's where my bike is."

"Why's it up there?"

"I told you, I'm going to ride my bike."

"You said you would jump over me."

"I will. On my bike."

"How?" she asked, suddenly standing up.

"I'm going to ride down that plank from the door, across this board, down this one, over this dirt, up this ramp and jump through the air over you, landing about here on the ground."

"Can I try after?"

"You're not big enough yet."

"Why not?"

"'Cause your only five and you have to be at least seven."

She was satisfied and lay down again.

"No," I said, "closer to the ramp."

She shuffled over to the right spot. Now everything was set.

I got my bike and pushed it to the open door. Looking down, I prepared myself by looking at where I had to ride. Then I started the commentary.

"Ladies and Gentlemen, Boys and Girls…"

"I can't see anything!" she shouted.

I yelled back, "Shut up…just look straight up and you'll see me fly over you…I'll tell you when I'm coming."

"Ladies and Gentlemen…"

"You already said that part."

"I know...shut up."

"Prepare to be amazed as Evil KerPluckrose races down the ramps of death and..."

"Who's dying?"

"Nobody...it's just the speech, now be quiet and lie still."

"...and over the young damsel below."

"Are you ready, young Damsel?"

Silence from below.

"That's you," I yelled, "are you ready?"

"Ready?"

"On with the show then. Stay still, here I come!"

With one push I was off, pedaling down the first plank, onto the flat one over the fence, still pedaling and picking up speed. Down the last board, over the dirt and up the ramp.

"NIGEL!" my mother screamed from the garage shed, just as I reached the top of the ramp and launched the bike into the air.

I had a huge smile on my face as I soared through the air, with a glance down, I saw Johanna safe below as I passed over top of her, then quickly looking over at Mom. She looked pale.

The ground came up to meet the bike before I had stopped looking at Mom. All I felt was this tremendous jerk as the bike handlebars were ripped from my hands. I suddenly stopped going down and shot back up again. My butt hurt suddenly. Something hard hit me in the chin. I hit the ground like a sack of potatoes. The bike wheel was spinning in front of me as my fingers went through the spokes.

Then the tip of my finger came off with a surprisingly quick pinch.

"Owww!" I cried grabbing my hand.

Mom started that noise that she made when she wanted my dad quickly, "G...Lynn."

She ran towards me. Johanna was already up.

"Can I try now?"

All I could do was look at the end of my finger. Mom was there now and Dad was coming at the run. The Gypsies sat on their wagon watching and waiting for the old lady inside.

Mom picked up the detached finger and Dad picked me up. The two of them raced me to the hospital. Nobody said anything.

When we arrived at the hospital, a nurse met us and quickly took us into a room in Emergency. The doctor came in and had a look.

"It's alright. We can put that back on. It's mostly just the fleshy part, no bone or nerve damage."

Mom started crying and the doctor suggested that maybe Dad should take her outside while he sewed me back on.

After they had gone he started to get everything ready with the nurse.

"Want to watch or go to sleep?" he asked.

"I can watch?"

"If you want."

"Will there be lots of blood?"

"Don't think so."

"Will it hurt?"

"Nah, I'll freeze your finger and you'll feel me pulling the stitches through. Gonna hurt later when the freezing comes out, but I'll give you some pills for that."

"I'll watch."

As he started to sew me back on to me, we had a nice conversation about what had happened. What my dad had said about protection and my mom yelling. Hadn't thought of that one. I didn't make a very good stuntman, as I hadn't thought of her distracting me or how hard the ground was.

What he was doing was very interesting though. I really paid attention to how he did this.

When he was done, he said, "Hold both your hands up."

I did as I was asked and he started to count the fingers on my right hand.

"Ten, nine, eight, seven, six," then looked at the other hand, "and five more are eleven. Good you have them all."

"Huh?" I said looking at them. He was right.

"Wait until you are older to be a stuntman, will you? I don't like sewing little boys back together."

"Yes sir."

He left and Mom and Dad came back in.

"Nigel," Mom said, "I don't like picking you up in two pieces. Please, please don't be a stuntman."

"I'm sorry, Mom. I changed my mind anyway."

"No more stuntman?"

"No. I think I want to be a doctor instead."

"No practicing and wait until you graduate university," my dad said quickly.

"Yes sir," I said with a grin.